Also by V.Y. Mudimbe

Shaba Deux: Les Carnets de
Soeur Marie-Gertrude

Déchirures (Torn Segments)

Entre les Eaux (Between the Waters)

Les Fuseaux Parfois
(Sometimes the Borders)

Carnet d' Amérique
(Notes on an American Trip)

L'Ecart (The Deviation novel)

L'Odeur du Père
(The Smell of the Father)

The Invention of Africa

vy Mudimbe

WITH A FOREWORD BY
JACQUES HOWLETT

TRANSLATED FROM THE FRENCH BY
MARJOLIJN DE JAGER

A FIRESIDE BOOK
PUBLISHED BY SIMON & SCHUSTER INC.
NEW YORK • LONDON • TORONTO
SYDNEY • TOKYO

BEFORE
THE
BIRTH
OF THE
MOON

Fireside
Simon & Schuster Building
Rockefeller Center
1230 Avenue of the Americas
New York, New York 10020

Originally published in France as *Le Bel Immonde* by
La Société Nouvelle Présence Africaine

FIRESIDE and colophon are registered trademarks
of Simon & Schuster Inc.

Designed by Diane Stevenson/SNAP·HAUS GRAPHICS
Manufactured in the United States of America

1   3   5   7   9   10   8   6   4   2

Library of Congress Cataloging in Publication Data
Mudimbe V. Y.
[Bel immonde. English]
Before the birth of the moon / V.Y. Mudimbe; with a foreword by
Jacques Howlett ; translated from the French
by Marjolijn de Jager.
p.   cm.
Translation of: Le bel immonde.
"A Fireside book."
I. Title
PQ3989.2.M77B413 1989   88-27459
843—dc19   CIP

ISBN 0-671-66840-4

ACKNOWLEDGMENTS

The translator wishes to express her sincere appreciation to M. Geoffrey Jones of Présence Africaine, Paris, for his efforts towards making the American translation rights available. Deep gratitude goes to her editor in New York, Malaika Adero, for her contagious enthusiasm and unfailing support for this work.

To V. Y. Mudimbe, with my deep respect and admiration,
M.d.J.

"Il vaut mieux, selon moi, faire sa part à l'époque, puisqu'elle la réclame si fort . . . Créer aujourd'hui, c'est créer dangereusement. Toute publication est un acte et cet acte expose aux passions d'un siècle qui ne pardonne rien. . . . La question . . . est seulement de savoir comment, parmi les polices de tant d'idéologies, (que d'églises, quelle solitude!) l'étrange liberté de la création reste possible."

—*Albert Camus*, Discours de Suède

FOREWORD

Grasp in what has been written a symptom
of what has been left unsaid.
—Nietzsche
Beyond Good and Evil

How can one not be sensitive to what has been appearing here and there for some time now in French-speaking Black African fiction: the question of power tends to occupy stage front.

In its most prominent manifestations, Black African literature written in French has always been a literature of warmth, engagement, criticism, and realism; not a literature of evasion, adventure, fantasy, or dreamworld; not—and even less so—a literature that contemplates its own literality, but a political literature in the broadest sense of the word.

With the same intentions, the preoccupations of a new generation of writers appear in the literature today. These are writers who are more attentive to the internal contradictions that Africa faces than to the revolts and the historic demands that incited their elders in earlier days. It's a different battle, the stakes of which are no less high since it concerns questioning the authority of power and, as far as it regards the citizens in general, strengthening their individuality, if not restoring their wounded identity.

In this narrative, the question of power is not tackled head on; the author applies himself above all to imagining the inner depths of one of those prestigious characters who are participants in the world of political power. We know more about his joys, his woes, and his thoughts as a private man than we do about his activities as a Minister of State or his speeches as a public official. This bias does not obscure the sociopolitical situation; quite the contrary (we are concerned with Zaire in 1965 and the story takes place in Kinshasa). From the psychological point of view, the story depends heavily on the social and political structures; it is, in fact, a noticeable characteristic of this narrative that it so inextricably and so fatally links individual destinies to the impersonal and con-

12

tradictory forces which torment the country; and that it approaches the malaise of consciences and the chaos of circumstances with such an all-encompassing grasp.

The other main character, a young woman, also finds herself jeopardized by the events—the rebellion—that shake the region. With history as backdrop, these two figures, at once both close to and distant from one another, overwhelm the reader with a sense of crisis, indeed of downfall, and above all of a fundamental ambiguity through their anticipation, their erring, and their destruction. Towards this end, in terms of the writing itself, the skillful shifts in perspective, the transitions within the plot, and the multiple variations of distance from the narrative concur and shape the whole.

From the start, the first sequence of the text (which consists of twenty sequences grouped in four sections of five each) bathes in this uncertain light. "She is waiting . . ." in the half-light of a nightclub. We are dealing with an almost contemplative prelude written in the third person. She, a woman of the sort normally termed dance hostess, absent-mindedly allows herself to be touched by an American, who is simple and clumsy, if you will. The description of the place and of what one comes to do there—drink, smoke, dance, purchase a body for the night—is shot through with visions as if from a dream; it is perforated with unusual snatches from a poem by Stefan George from his collection *Der Stern des Bundes*, a text full of Nietzschean echoes that evoke the superman, the seer, the initiated one, the new Lord, "alone of his rank"; a rare text which doubtless does not repeat itself by chance in the dreamy consciousness of this young woman, who—another ambiguity—prefers the completeness of love discovered in the arms of a woman friend to the vulgar desire of men.

Who is she, this young woman, most often presented to us in the cold perspective established by the use of the third person, or challenged according to the otherness/intimacy and the evocation/invocation of the second person? (Her "I" does not intervene until the third and fourth sequences of the last chapter when the die is cast!) What fantasies, what complexes, what avatars of domination does she represent?

Here arises the question of the African subject writing today, the analysis of which remains to be done. The symptomatic effect of this woman's character is, in any event, very strong and, furthermore, her existential reality imposes itself in a most convincing manner throughout the book. On the level of an unsophisticated reading, this feminine pole of the book is that of passivity, sensuality, fickleness, and of a certain innocent perversity.

Opposite the ambiguous beauty, there is the strong breadth of the wealthy and powerful man, the Minister of State. He is a complex character, cold and lucid, cynical if need be, restless, and capable of authentic feelings. He loves his young son, and he is deeply disturbed by the sense of freedom, at once spiritual and physical, with which the young courtesan inspires him. A subtle relationship is established between the conquered master and his willing and enigmatic slave. They form an impure couple, unclean in the religious sense of the word, who will be shattered by the impersonal forces of the police and the political power structure. Although not stated in the text, it is as if, one might think, this scandalous duo revealed a certain form of authenticity (that of the "new lords"?) in relationship to the reigning "order." Who is unclean? The strong and the beautiful or the blind ruling order?

The Minister, caught in the deadly game of political forces and obedient to the terrible gravity of the occult powers held by the traditional leaders, will end up "liquidated," sacrificed to the State's cause. The young woman, saved by her passivity, will emerge alive from the trap set by the police. She remains a lovely, disillusioned appearance, a poetic whore, black jewel of the expensive bars: "You are good looking, my technician... Entertain me. All right? Let's dance . . . "; ludicrous!

Thus, these two beings, devoted to life and the enjoyment thereof, end up vanquished by the forces of circumstances, two pitiful marionettes.

From these brief remarks, the reader will have understood that in this narrative, V. Y. Mudimbe takes a certain distance from the subject matter which he treats. No technique is ingenuous; the one that unfolds its virtuosity here partakes of the significance of the story; what appears together with the implicit question of power is a sophisticated novelistic discourse, a certain way of storytelling that is more ascetic than in most African texts so that indirection is preferred to immediacy, distantiation to participation, and vision and accuracy to effusiveness.

In this original literary undertaking from Zaire, what is finally brilliantly demonstrated is the demand for new forms of mastery, not only in the telling, but even more so in its creation.

Jacques Howlett

BEFORE
THE
BIRTH
OF THE
MOON

INTRODUCTION

Be prudent and say no more. Don't you
understand what it is that now causes you to collide
with misfortunes of your own making and what it
is that follows upon such ignominy? You have
brought more than your share of unhappiness upon
yourself.

—Sophocles

And the scribes and the Pharisees brought
unto him a woman taken in adultery; and when they had set
her in the midst, they said unto him, Master, this woman was
taken in adultery, in the very act.

Now Moses in the law commanded us that such
should be stoned: but what sayest thou? This they said,
tempting him, that they might have to accuse him.

But Jesus stooped down, and with his finger wrote on the ground, as though he heard them not. So when they continued asking him, he lifted up himself and said unto them: He that is without sin among you, let him first cast a stone at her. And again he stooped down on the ground.

—The Gospel according to St. John

I

1

She is waiting. Every evening the same. Eyes half-closed, she smiles while her right hand lazily caresses her silk scarf. She is always hoping, looking for her lord and master, visibly impassioned and at the same time spent by this invasion of music which entangles her in a sea of cigarette smoke and the stale smell of alcohol. She

would have liked to be dancing; to be clinging to Stefan
George, to be convinced of the mystery of her own heart so
that she could enter joyfully into the death of lyrics, so well-
preserved by the life of a melody:

> *Don't judge them by their swords or thrones:*
> *All notables, of any rank, still have*
> *a coarse and carnal eye*
> *the same raw look of the leering beast . . .*

On the dance floor, the dancers are clutching each
other. She is watching them. The men are holding the women as
closely as if it were a last farewell. She lets herself go as well. An
American is at work on her. Fresh polish, bright colors, her
eyes suddenly joyful, she sings along with the orchestra:

> *Far from the tree's trunk, away in the brush*
> *grows the rare shoot, alone of its kind.*
> *And you recognize your kindred*
> *by the pure light in their eyes . . .*

He is talking to her. Startled, she focuses on his
somewhat entreating, slightly unhappy voice. Why not go
with her right away? He does not understand that she would
be so resistant to money, unfolds an enormous handkerchief
and wipes his face. She looks at him, searches his eyes, then
bursts out laughing. Will she give in? She knows these eyes,
the eyes of a beaten or a soaked dog. She is in control. Once

BEFORE THE BIRTH OF THE MOON

she gives herself, she knows that she has nothing to counter with if she wants to earn her reward: she will be the one with the ravaged eyes.

Amused, she follows the hand that shyly manipulates her thighs. It is a hairy hand. The too-weak light makes it look like tortoiseshell. The veins stand out, like conquerors. She raises her glass to eye level; watchfully she contemplates the ice cubes shimmering like diamonds in the whiskey. She smiles, pleased, and directs her gaze into a dark corner. A couple. Just like them: an American and a black woman. She lights a cigarette, takes two drags one right after the other. A slow dance. He looks at her. She puts out her cigarette.

"Shall we dance?"

"Yes."

He clings to her, imprisons her. The lights are lowered. They hold each other closely. A melody comes up, all-embracing.

> . . . *When my grave's tombstone is unsealed*
> *to receive a second occupant,*
> *since the tomb, too, will have learned*
> *the way that women have of serving as*
> *bed to many more than one alone . . .*

"Are you happy?"

"Sure, and you?"

He has to take a deep breath. Perhaps it is his whiskey breath. She withdraws her head slightly, then rests it on

25

his shoulder. It is so intoxicating, you said one day—do you remember that?—a smell of tree stumps burnt by alcohol fumes. It is the smell of America. You smile. No doubt won over again by the revelations of dancing with a stranger.

They barely move. Just like the others. Another light goes out, a new patch of intimacy settles in. Bodies seek each other.

> . . . *And when the gravedigger sees*
> *this luminous bracelet of hair*
> *shining around bone*
> *will he not want to leave us in peace*
> *thinking that here lie . . .*

"What do you do in life?"
"I'm an American."
"Yes, I can see that. But your profession?"
"I'm a technician."
"You're a good dancer."

He has his hands on your hips. His arms are creeping vines, forming a double hyphen between you. Only your shoulders navigate across the barely perceptible rolling.

> . . . *two lovers who believed thus to find*
> *a way for their souls to meet*
> *amidst the throng of the Judgement Day*
> *and to linger just a little while*
> *inside this tomb . . .*

"Still happy?"

"Yes, indeed. Except for the heat. I'm dying in here. What's your name?"

"That really matters to you? Why don't you tell me about your country?"

"America?"

A huge white bay opens up, protected by the police. Absentmindedly, you come across enormous and impenetrable ships. A chorus of rivers. Spectacular and wild mountains parade with entire movie houses as their floats. And so all his anecdotes begin to flutter about on the last strains of a gloomy melody:

> . . . *You shall be something like Mary Magdalen*
> *and I some other saint, at the same time*
> *we'll be adored by every woman*
> *and by a few, a very few men . . .*

Brutally, the light comes on again. A cha-cha-cha encircles it immediately. Your American smiles protectively and takes you by the shoulders.

"Thank you, my nameless little girl."

"It was nice, wasn't it?"

"Yes, indeed. I like the words. Do you know the writer?"

"No. Why?"

"Haven't you been to school?"

"Of course I have! I speak French don't I?"

27

Disaster. He is speaking to you of German, English, American writers who bore you. Suddenly, you skid to a halt, happy; there is a smile on your lips for her who is coming towards you. He stops his lecture, too, so that he can undress her with his eyes, and it shows. She is wearing a short, two-toned, yellow-orange dress, very low-cut. You admire once more the lovely outline of her eyebrows, and her teeth almost blue in the luminous play of the neon lights. Hurriedly, she whispers in your ear:

"You'll come and get me tomorrow morning at ten?"

"At the usual place?"

"Yes, if that's all right."

His right hand under your skirt, he is fascinated watching the new arrival head towards the bar.

"Is she a friend of yours?"

"No, that's my sister."

"She is pretty."

"Isn't she though?"

And you burst out laughing. She, your sister! After all, to the Europeans as to the Americans, all Blacks look alike. It is so much easier to let her be your sister.

~

It had been a rainy afternoon. You were feeling lonely, sad. She came, spoke to you, ushered you into her life. What, in fact, were you looking for in that little store, in that seedy neighborhood? Some fabric or a dress? She discouraged you in order to teach you how to cheat. Just a little bit, like everyone else. Fabrics? She told you they were horribly expensive.

28

"In this store there is more of a choice than you can possibly imagine. Only the prices . . . Come and see for yourself. This style for example, isn't it nice? No? Look at this lovely flesh-colored sheath . . . And this little light suit, that's not bad at all now, is it? How much? A fortune, my dear, a small fortune. That little white number there, next to the blue shirt and blouse, what do you think of that one? The boss, he's Greek, sells off more than half of his stock on the black market. I'm the one who finds him the saleswomen to move the stuff. A real stroke of luck, this job. Come, let's go have a drink. Will you help me? Yes? You'll see: you'll have everything you want . . ."

"What's your name? You're right, that's not important at all. You'll be my little sister, is that all right?"

At this point, you worshipped her, you were converted, convinced that your love for her was a permanent state of rapture, as remote from the male as it was from any regret. Your queasy faintheartedness at the beginning had quickly disappeared in the glow of the unsettling infectiousness in which you had recognized the ecstasy of your childhood. You still remember the artlessness of her spontaneity: "I love you. Very much. Just to live with you. To meet after work. Don't you feel this need for a pure, luminous spot of shade, a hiding place far from masculine excretions? Do you love me just a little? Me, I already adore you. Drink your tomato juice . . . Isn't it good? Be sweet, lift your head a little so that I can marvel at your lovely throat . . ."

She is at the bar, luxuriating in the masculine frustrations and desire elicited by her body. She will go out with her American and offer him her loins.

Filled with hate, you discover another American at work on your thighs. You are thinking that he is defiling you. His hand is so far removed from your innocence of yesterday, of all the days past and yet to come. How far it is, too, from the delights and the discreet depths of your shared womanhood. And this evening, as always, you wonder if, despite everything, you ought to continue holding on to this stroke of luck which throws your senses off every single time.

She empties her glass. Her friend is talking to her. She laughs and her teeth flash in the light as it turns bluer, while the music fades a little. Right at this very moment you would like to feel them against your own. Roughly you close your legs and get up.

"Leave me alone. You're hurting me."

"I'm sorry, truly I . . ."

He seems shocked. In one gulp he empties his glass of whiskey, then goes on to find another girl.

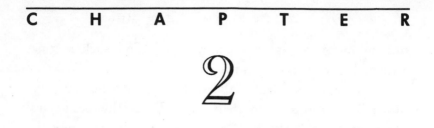

C H A P T E R

2

ou have picked the man for you. He is large, well nourished. A brilliant politician. You have known him a long time. Do you love him? Why do you go back to him with such regularity? In the long run, won't your revulsion necessarily slip into the struc-

31

BEFORE THE BIRTH OF THE MOON

ture of his demands? But can you still find such sacrifice acceptable for the love of a man?

One day, she had confided: "They're all the same with that feline expression in their eyes. Especially politicians. They are tigers." She had taken your hands, was pressing them while looking you straight in the eyes. "... They take you, size you up, crush you mercilessly, then abandon you. You must always come and see me afterwards. Together, so that we can forget it all, we'll try to live our little bit of carefully collected happiness..." She had placed your left hand on her right breast. A few moments only. You were reading her eyes, tenderly. Your hand had begun to tremble on her chest. Shaken, you had whispered: "They nauseate me. It's an ugly thing, really, a man." And while she, naked, was loving your body, you were thinking, shamefully, of your profession.

A messy profession among a great many others. The mechanic, the metalworker, or the coal miner come home just as dirty from their work. Like you. But you? The important thing is afterwards, she told you, to find the calm that leads to abandon and forgetfulness.

You look at him. A handsome man. A beautiful shade of black. Physically powerful. Fawn-colored eyes that bespoke a quiet patience. The fingers of his left hand are steadily tapping a glass, one after the other, a bit mad. The product of a new era: Secretary of State once, Minister three times. Malicious gossip claims that he insists on being called

"Excellency" and on being addressed in the third person only. What does it matter! Usually you call him "Eminence" just as a joke, and he has never objected. Your eyes are shining. You ask him:

"Shall we dance?"

"No, little one. I am tired."

You'll wait. It is only normal. In this country one is born tired. The sun, no doubt. One truth like another. Like the one that sustains your patience at this very moment: African politicians have a playful generosity; they spend money more easily than American technicians. So you submit yourself. He loves little scandals and begs of you:

"Were you here yesterday when they arrested that captain who was dressed like a woman?"

"Yes, why?"

"Tell me about it. The story interests me."

You smile, annoyed. A stupid story. The American had also wanted to hear it in every detail. When you first saw her, about ten days ago, you had said to yourself: Look, a new one. Her makeup is beautiful. She surrounded herself in mystery, pointlessly provoking the men. The first few days you were a little envious of her: she had personality. When she danced she was truly dazzling. As time went on, her success began to get you down. Last night, an American who was dancing with her must have made a sudden movement.

"How?"

"I don't know. You know how it is when you're

33

dancing . . . In any event, one of her breasts rolled on the floor."

"A breast?"

"Well, a falsie, obviously."

A hit song breaks loose. In a flash the dance floor fills up. Gestures begin to mimic rhythm. You would really like to dance.

"Shall we dance?"

"No, no, no. I told you I was tired. Why don't you order another drink. Who actually arrested him?"

"I haven't the faintest idea. Cops from Security it seems."

"Were there a lot of them?"

"That I can't tell you. You know, once there is a raid . . . Come on now, you're beginning to bother me . . . Was I supposed to hang around and count them? They're plain-clothes, you know. . . ."

"Really?"

"Anyway, there are always a lot of them here. The one who is talking with the two girls at the bar, for instance. And in the corner there, right across from us, the fat one who is kissing that girl . . . And the one on my left, the awkward, skinny one who's drinking by himself, I think he's one of them also . . ."

You are observing him, your brute of a man. Are you so sure that nothing about him appeals to you? And yet, you find him likeable, this slob, as your girlfriend calls him. His fondness—love, he calls it—weighs upon you heavily as his

BEFORE THE BIRTH OF THE MOON

unending questions annoy you. His political career, in which he takes such pride, does not impress you. You simply wished that a friendly complicity could be established between you that could make of your interest in his wealth a less intense passion. But how? He is so carefully tuned in to himself and to his own accomplishments.

"How is your wife?"

"What?"

"Your wife, is she all right?" He frowns, a bit taken aback, hesitates, then answers vaguely, his voice barely audible:

"I think so."

You are able to think of her without fear or jealousy. This is your strength, and it is exactly this which troubles him. He is perfectly willing to admit that you know about her. But that you ask after her health at every turn! He dutifully drinks his whiskey. You are daydreaming. You think you understand why you tolerate him. But that he claims to love you strikes you as extraordinary. There is a shift in the music. Is that your stomach tightening? A vague smile which you interpret.

"Dance?"

"Yes, if you really want to."

The lights are dimmed slightly. You like this return to darkness that allows bodies to enact a game as inoffensive as it is pleasurable. In his eyes you discover a burnt-sugar sweetness, and it reminds you of the faces you made as a young high-school girl in love. He is gliding along and you are clinging to him. Moustaki.

Dance as much as you can
dance around the earth
free as a fish in the water
free as a bird in the
air...

His arms are in a stranglehold. He is barely moving and you begin to notice the heat that rises from his body.

"What have you been up to since the day before yesterday? Whom have you seen?"

The ritual question. In the beginning you would get defensive, wondering what right he had to regulate your free hours as he does your encounters with him. But now you are almost waiting for this question of his. It indicates continuity. It proves to you that nothing has changed. And, as usual, you play games. You tell him of the government ministers and the parliamentarians whom you have met by whatever chance the evenings offered, knowing perfectly well that you are irritating him even as you arouse his curiousity. Nothing frightens you any longer. You are in charge once again.

...Light as the wind dancing in the trees
or the mast of a ship dancing under a wave
dance as much as you can
on the pavement on the grass
on the table of a pub
in the shade of taverns...

36

He is perspiring. You inhale a smell that mixes sweat, toilet soap, and cologne. His fingers are pressing down your ribs and you notice him breathing heavily down your neck. Make him talk.

"You all right?"

"Yes. How about you?"

"All right . . ."

Make him talk at any cost. Otherwise you will soon be leaving. You would like to dance some more. To live. To feel your body melt into the music.

> . . . *Dance just as we live, dance just as we love*
> *dance just as we write poems on walls*
> *dance as much as you can*
> *dance around the earth* . . .

You can already see the rapid unrolling of things to come. Your stomach feels hollow. You wonder what you can do to stop time, to be frozen in the dying melody. The lights come up again, roughly, and there is the invitation you were expecting:

"Shall we leave?"

"Already?"

"Yes, I'm dead tired."

What a joke! He is dead tired, he says. Outta Season invades the room: *I've been loving you too long*. You are groaning at the mere thought of having that song in your head until tomorrow evening. It's always the same story. You never know how to leave, how to stop. Against your will you gather up your purse, your cigarettes, your lighter. He is dead tired, he says. And yet, as always, he will not leave you until dawn. You are whistling *I've been loving you too long*. He looks at you insistently. You think you understand: he is already living what is yet to come, happy with the prospect. Half raised up on his elbows he will reign, he will crush you, while you, eyes closed as always, will count the minutes of your ordeal. A sound of the sea's undertow rises in your chest. Barely outside, you suddenly feel unhappy and very meekly you observe: "It's really chilly tonight."

$$3$$

She smiled at her as soon as she recognized her. The other responded in kind. Both of them had dark circles under their eyes, tired faces. She offered her a cigarette. It was refused.

"Things not going well?"

"No, I'm just exhausted, that's all."

"Shall we take a cab?"

"No, please. Let's walk. I feel like walking. I think that'll do me good."

Ten o'clock in the morning. The city was full of people. She takes her hand. They begin to walk: two good little girls walking quietly along the avenues. The shop windows don't appeal to them at all. They go down the Boulevard du 30 Juin; then, around Bata, they begin their climb up to the Great Market.

"What happened?"

"Nothing. Not really anything. Well, nothing special."

"Is he pestering you, this politician of yours?"

"As always. He wears me out, but . . ."

"Don't tell me you're in love!"

"No, that isn't it."

A faint smile appears. The pressing of her hand? As they reach the Memling Hotel, taxi drivers first whistle at them, then accost them verbally with blunt and obvious vulgarities. They're an easy target. They laugh it off and continue to push through the middle of a crowd that grows more and more dense. The poor were climbing up with the sun to attack the rich, European section of town. Multicolored waves, all cries, noise, song, and laughter. So as not to lose each other in this flow, they hold each other by the waist.

"So what about your politician? You were saying . . ."

"I don't feel like seeing him anymore."

"That's not very hard. Send him on his way."

Sure, nothing would be easier. However, what do you say to make him understand? He is convinced that he'll hold you through his generosity, and he has never stopped to think about the significance of your sickened renunciations. And for your part, you're also hiding from yourself the bitter pleasure which he does occasionally bring you.

"Aren't you going to say anything?"

"I think I'll write him a note. That's easier. It will avoid having to explain things."

"You're right. You know, for quite a while now I've been saying to myself that you weren't doing well . . ."

"No, don't say that. He is kind. A bit clinging, a little too garish maybe, but kind. Yes, really kind: a big, rather lovable teddy bear."

She looks at you in surprise; won't take her eyes off you. You sense it. As a result, you grow more anxious about your feelings, wonder by what right she, too, wants to dictate your relationships at any cost. A dark flash, a sad glimmer runs suddenly across your eyes. The world totters. If only you could sleep as much as you'd like, until dusk. Sleep would allow oblivion.

Once home, you threw yourself on the bed, discouraged and in tears. She came to you, tender, motherly, took you in her arms and spoke to you. ". . . You're tired. Upset. It's nothing terrible. Just exhaustion. Yes, rest now, just rest. Go to sleep. Otherwise you'll become restless. Just let yourself go. Rest up, take a few days off. Sure, and don't feel guilty about it. What good would it do to kill yourself for

41

these pigs? Tell me, what earthly good? They're just tools. You're not going to sacrifice yourself for a tool, for God's sake. Stretch out your legs. All the way. Yes, there you go. Isn't that better?" She made you drink some scalding hot tea, then gently undressed you.

You were dozing off when, in a haze, you saw her get up to open the window. The air came in bringing a strong wave of heat along with it. You saw her struggle. She was catching her breath. When she came back, she leaned against the wall for a moment, then came to sit on the bed, distraught. You asked her what was wrong.

"I don't know. Dizziness. It happens more and more often. It lasts for a few moments, then goes away."

"You should see the doctor."

"Yes. I'll go this afternoon."

The room is a tiny, uncomfortable place. A large double bed fills it almost entirely. To the left is an old wardrobe which serves both as closet and as medicine cabinet; to the right, right next to a door that opens onto a minuscule bathroom, is a wooden box that holds an oil burner and takes up whatever space there is.

Once her little sister fell asleep, she got up, pushed the door to the bathroom and rushed inside. Mechanically, she began to scrape the whitewashed walls with her fingers, very conscientiously, then checked all the casings underneath the sink and along the walls. Tense, a hunted animal, she returned to the room, opened the wardrobe as quietly as she could, starting with the medicine cabinet, searching one box

42

after another, jar after jar. Then she attacked the clothes: she took out one dress after another, feeling each one by hand, inch by inch. At the end of two hours, she got up, poured herself a stiff glassful of whiskey and drank it down in one gulp. Dejected, drops of sweat covering her face, hands shaking with exhaustion, she patiently put each item back in its place and went into the bathroom.

She stood still in front of the mirror. Her somber hazel eyes were tired, her thin face haggard. She leaned down on the sink to take off her wig: a somewhat prominent forehead appeared, dominating all of her face. With her index finger she caressed two wrinkles brought out by her fatigue. Just to sleep, she thought, just to sleep for a few hours. Once she had some rest, she could go to see the doctor. Probably towards the end of the afternoon. Yes, I'll certainly feel better by then . . . She was just letting her skirt slip down when she heard a knocking at the door. On tiptoe she ran to open it.

"Sir?"

"Police."

"What do you want from me?"

"Do you live alone?"

"No, I live with a friend. What do you want?"

He was calm, looked her up and down with scornful indifference. She was convinced she was the innocent victim of an error. Frantic thoughts ran together in her head and just as quickly dislodged themselves again.

"Where is your friend?"

"She's asleep."

"At this hour! Wake her up."

He had grabbed her by the shoulders, was pushing her gently but firmly back into the room. Like lightning, a thought crossed her mind. She realized that, because of her friend's love life, she was perhaps a participant in some serious events. With her hand she awkwardly wiped away the sweat that was suddenly covering her face. She considered throwing herself on her knees and pleading, and turned towards the police officer with a sad look. She caught a sparkle of cold attention in his eyes, almost hatred already, as is customary with those who have the power to pronounce on the life and death of others. She bent over the bed: "Ya, Ya, wake up. Ya, wake up now."

She half opened her eyes, saw him, a tree towering straight up into the air at the foot of her bed; and she asked without surprise:

"Who is this?"

"Police. Please wake up!"

"Why?"

"Ya, I really don't know. What about you, don't you have any idea what the police might want from us?"

She was watching her, worried and probing at the same time. The door creaked. She barely turned around, two men were entering the room. They were plainclothes men. Like the first one, they were stocky, in dark suits, dark glasses, a familiar look. One of the newcomers rapidly spoke a few words to the first one, then froze to attention at his left side while the other took the right. She knelt down by the side of the bed, embraced Ya for a long time in order to overcome the fear mounting inside her. Between her fingers she tightly clutched the small medallion of the Virgin that hung around her friend's neck, and murmured:

"Don't be afraid, Ya. I'm here. We're together. I'll never betray you. Never, Ya. Do you understand that?"

Stretched out on her back, her left arm alongside her body, the right one around the shoulders of her friend who was now sobbing with her head on Ya's chest, Ya looked at them. Her numbed brain wanted to understand, but she could not manage to link two coherent ideas together. Police? She had her doubts. In her opinion, they looked like hardened pimps or deposed politicians. Murderers' faces. Of what could they be accused? She was staring at them meekly, in terror. There they were, all three of them, as rigid as justice itself, almost too neat in their new suits. She told herself that these men had nothing but disgust for them and their seedy little room. Break through, she thought, break through this atmosphere of anguish. No matter how.

With a sudden movement Ya lifted sheet and blanket, left the hollow of her bed and went, completely naked, towards the bathroom.

"Stop!" they yelled at her.

"Wait till I get dressed. I'll be with you in a minute."

At almost the same time she was aware of someone running and then a blow. Her temples exploded. She found herself on the floor. She saw him there in front of her. His legs spread, hands in his pockets; he had taken off his glasses, showing inscrutable, slightly mocking eyes. He was dealing her light kicks, particularly in the ribs and the belly. Neatly, as if he were trying not to dirty himself. Cries came forth. She no longer heard the moaning of her friend. The pain grew larger. Mental torture. Physical burns. Her ribs were opening up. She knew that the motions she made to protect her face were laughable. It was then that she began to howl like a lunatic.

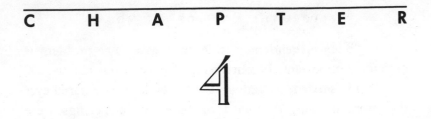

4

Three dry raps of the President's small gavel half awakened him, caused him to make a sudden movement: his right elbow slipped and snapped lightly against the armrest of the chair. It hurt him and he woke up completely. The President of the Commission of National Defense was speaking.

"Silence, gentlemen. Silence, please. The problem is extremely important. It concerns the future of our nation . . ."

He sniffed, looked around the table, encountered eyes that were dozing, distracted or bored. Whisperings were floating in the air. Conscientiously, he went back to his daydreams. His eyes staring at the garland of small shimmering globes hanging in the archway, he was obstinately bringing a face back to life. He was unreeling the alleys in bloom where he would encounter, stage by stage and at the appointed time, each one of the habits of the beloved. And within this sweet drowsiness he followed the report of the Secretary of the Commission on the internal situation of the country.

"According to the information we have from National Security, all rebel centers are organized along one single pattern, the main rules of which are: first, a clear separation between the military and the civil organization; second, the formation of the villagers into regiments for all military actions; third, . . ."

Now he was drawing circles, interlaced designs, and thinking of the irrational act he had committed the previous weekend: taking her to a motel on the outskirts of Kinshasa. He could have run into one of his numerous acquaintances at any moment; or even the Sunday afternoon when he had driven her to the swimming hole, he could have met his children who came to bathe there from time to time. He had left it up to chance to make or break things. And everything had been wonderful.

His eyes had become cheerful. He smiled at his

48

friend, the Vice-President of the Chamber of Representatives, sitting across from him, who responded with a wink of complicity and continued to puff on his pipe, his eyes drooping. The voice of the Secretary flagged from weariness.

"The civil organization consists of three main structures, formed along strongly hierarchical lines and, it seems, very strictly compartmentalized: the General Directorate devises the manner of recruitment, programs the instruction of the membership, oversees public justice, controls the monies, centralizes intelligence and arms. Immediately below this leadership body comes the Regional Committee, also known by the rebels as the Sector Directorate. It is precisely a level of action: it brings together certain people who are responsible for verifying that directives received are completed. The last level is that of the village: a committee of fanatics, known as the 'revolutionary committee,' assures the involvement of the villagers.

"Gentlemen, in the files that you have been given you will find biographical records of a few of the leaders of this movement. Kindly consult them . . ."

Like the others, he leafed through the slips, stopping every now and then to look at this face or that one. In passing, he recognized two of his former governmental colleagues. He realized that his hands were perspiring, wiped them off. It was past noon. The Secretary's voice shot out:

"Are there any questions?"

Almost instinctively he raised his hand. He stood up, caught his breath, cleared his throat, and spoke firmly:

49

"Your report, Mr. Secretary, is extraordinary. But I take the liberty to tell you, on behalf of my colleagues here and on my own behalf, that the administrative, political, social or judiciary organization of these bandits may be of interest to the sociologists . . . What we would like to know is the geographical extent of this evil, the approximate number of these killers, and the measures to be taken to bring this calamity under control in the shortest possible time . . ."

He looked around the table and encountered nods of approval. Satisfied, he sat down again. The Secretary's voice was getting lost in the haze. "I am coming to that and, subsequently, with special permission from the Ministers of Justice and of the Interior, two of the rebels will be interrogated in your presence." His speech had excited him. He loosened his tie a little. He took a blank sheet of paper and, while the Secretary's voice, a small whirring sound, continued to hold forth, he began to write.

My friend,

My very dear, tender, and charming friend. I am thinking of grace itself. It has your face, is embodied in the look in your eyes. A prisoner of my own limitations, I would so like to believe that through you I might steadily discover, as if by chance, a meaning in your joy. It is a joy of the most everyday occurrence, of the simplest kind, the one which your presence radiates and which so pleasantly entices me.

I know you to be an exceptional person in that I think you will understand my fear of losing you. It often paralyzes me to the point of being unable to fully enjoy your presence. If, as they say, love means an integration of thoughts, the fulfillment of an encounter, then I must recognize—to my great sorrow!—that we have not yet reached that point. What unites us is rather the expression of secondhand ecstasies. I accept, oh yes, I do accept the enchantment of these moments, which are as rare as they are extraordinary, and the essential quality of which, perhaps even the only one, is that it helps me to live with the colorlessness of my marriage without drama or tension. All told, the circumspection of our meetings is in itself a negation of any high-flown sentiments. After all, what would we do with high-flown sentiments? I imagine you remaining as you are, free of all involvement, and I find it perfectly normal that I remain a prisoner of my ambitions and my success . . .

I am thinking that at this very moment you must . . .

The raw stridency of the voice of the Secretary of the Commission made him jump. He stopped writing and saw a man and a woman come in, followed by an officer of the judiciary police and by two armed soldiers.

"Through the special authority of the Ministers of Justice and of the Interior," the Secretary began again, "the judiciary officers will interrogate before you these accused, both of them officers of the rebel army. In conclusion, you will thus have a complete picture of the problems that concern us."

The man was tall and wretched-looking. Faded shirt and pants. Shaggy hair, swollen lips, his hands tied behind

51

his back, his feet bare. He did not look vicious, but seemed rather improbably vulnerable. He stared at the floor with the eyes of a fish on dry land.

"You stand accused as a rebel leader. Do you admit this?"

"Yes."

"What was your function in the rebellion?"

"At first I was a representative of the popular masses. In January 1964 I was promoted to group commander. I was responsible for a company of soldiers and for a female company of three hundred troops."

"Where was your base?"

"Nkata and Luende-Nzagala, from where I directed several operations."

"Was Luende-Nzagala your last base?"

"No. I left that post in October 1964. My superiors sent me to Dibanda. From there I was transferred to Sambo, to the General Directorate."

"And then?"

"After that we were camped in the forest of Ingetshi."

"Can you tell us what kind of weapons your supreme commander has at his disposal?"

"Five Fals, of which one is in bad shape, three Mauser 52's, four Mauser 36's; nineteen other Mausers are at the disposal of regional commanders; six Sten guns, six revolvers, and one Mauser in each subdirectorate."

"And you expect to conquer the regular army with that?"

"Yes. We have faith, that is what matters."

"It seems that your chief commander has a foreign specialist available to him, who supplies him with cartridges. Is that true?"

"He has a specialist, that is true; but he's not a foreigner."

"Who makes the rifles that the rebels use?"

"A group of our own young workers."

The Secretary had fallen asleep during the interrogation. His neighbor to the right awakened him with a light nudge of the elbow. He gave a brief order to the officer, who pushed the young woman forward. The President of the Commission was wearing his perpetual bony smile. The whispering grew stronger when this child was introduced. "Shock troops . . . Commander . . . Massacre of the villagers . . . Directly contributed to the destruction of several military details . . . Dangerous woman . . ." He saw her profile. A kid. Fifteen or sixteen? Maybe eighteen, twenty at the very most. Sunken cheeks. A dress of rough burlap which made her look unnecessarily ugly. An emaciated face. The large, steady eyes of a high school girl who had grown up too quickly. A challenge, he thought, as he watched her carefully.

He thought of his unfinished letter, tried to pick it up again where he left off, then put it aside in order to listen to the accused, the young girl who was answering with unprecedented candor.

"Are you a member of the so-called Revolutionary Democratic Movement?"

"Yes, for the past two years."

"Your rank in this movement?"

"Commander."

Leaning back slightly in his seat, the Secretary was stroking his small, finely shaped mustache. He seemed completely lost in his daydreams. The officer of the judiciary police was playing the macho: he was trying to trump up a rage, yelling, hammering the table with his fist.

"Commander! Dear commander! Instead of attending class, you are playing the little soldier, aren't you? How many men have you killed, you and your band of murderers?"

At times the girl would stiffen, then once again relaxed, she would continue to respond in a weary voice. "Were you living in the bivouac of Mubinzienne where you were arrested?"

"I've been living there for three months. Before that I was at the camp of Sambo."

"Why do you belong to this movement?"

"I came into it in order to learn to make pots and dishes. The boys in my village had told me that the Movement was teaching this."

"In the forest? Why flee from the military then?"

"I don't know."

"You are lying, aren't you?"

"Yes, I am lying. Just as you wish."

"Who forced you to go into the underground?"

"Men."

"What was your work in the bivouac? You don't really

54

think that we believe you were making pottery there! How many women were there?"

He looked at his watch. It was one-fifteen. The President of the Commission, he thought, is going well beyond the call of duty. It will be worth knowing what he has up his sleeve, he thought. The girl was getting on his nerves. She's wasting our time. In what way is she a threat to the state? Either she was a traitor or she was lying with extraordinary artlessness.

"I am hiding nothing. At the bivouac of Mubinzienne there were six of us girls, specialized in the art of stealing weapons from the military."

"How?"

"By disguising ourselves, for one thing."

They departed to the great pleasure of the majority of the Commission's membership. The President took the floor again, spoke of vigilance and of proposals to be submitted to the attention of the government. Files, portfolios, briefcases had already been closed. The members of the Commission were waiting politely. . .

5

It is hot. The radio is blaring. A craze of my wife's. The collapse of the government barely concerns me. I have been expecting it. What is it that all my friends are so terribly upset about? I should have taken the phone off the hook, just to be alone. Sitting on the terrace for a bit of fresh air, I force myself to read and am continually annoyed by the steady stream of sweat that drenches me and by the short, mysterious flickerings that shimmer in front of my eyes every so often.

I hear the children yelling in the yard. At one and the same time, their metallic voices both subdue and irritate me. Soon they will be going back to school. I shall have some peace and be able to take a nap at long last. Tomorrow, I'll pick up my links with life again. With my former State Department. Settling current affairs. What an irony!

What truly constrains me is not this downfall. That is a lie. Like the courtesies: "Minister of State . . . Your Excellency . . . Dear Sir, I was unpleasantly surprised to learn that the government . . . If you could only know how distraught I am . . . Yes, dear sir, I had the opportunity and the great fortune to have dealings with you . . . I know your ability . . . Yes, absolutely, you must come and see us . . . Our Party is counting fully on your vitality . . ." Certainly, this collapse took me by surprise. Nevertheless, it liberates me, gives me the opportunity to be a bit more free. More available to you. You haunt me. You must understand how enjoyable it is to have the possibility of wondering about you at my leisure.

I would never have believed that one day a love affair could have destroyed me to this extent. Perhaps I have been too naive, once again, by not concerning myself sufficiently with you in the face of my own desire. In the moist heat of this afternoon without end, it seems to me that our meeting of last night, like all our earlier encounters, forced itself upon me like a plunder, negating the feelings that I have for you. Yesterday, the look in your eyes was badly disguised and in it I saw a sadness and a hatred that presented me with intentions so phony, so beyond any acceptable limit, that I can only think they are expedient to you. In any event, you carry it off very well. It even makes you more beautiful.

Now that I think of it, what seems most damaging to me is the careful but brutal barrier that you have suddenly erected between us. Twice yesterday, I wondered if I, like all your other occasional partners, was not foisting myself upon you so openly that you have to fight back against the unlikely temptation to sacrifice yourself. On the whole, you want to be nothing more than an immense void vis-à-vis other people. Their clamor for you as much as their brutishness salvages your dreams, fills up your wallet, while justifying your contempt for them at the same time.

Calm down, I won't go back on my word. You are and will remain for me whatever you want it to be. Does one ask of much-loved clothes to be anything other than what they are? Just this one thing: I am uncomfortable every time I meet you. I know that my generosity diverts you as much as it appeals to you. I also know that you enjoy judging those of my kind and my rank through me. You suspect that, before I met you, it did occur that I would come apart in front of a woman. Each time it was a fresh surprise, a pleasant one.

58

They did not subjugate me. But you . . . I realize that, in and of itself, enslavement is neither a defect nor an illness. For you I would gladly accept it, if at least I were certain that it would not distress you by disturbing the full circle of your misery.

You see, I suspect that you want to carry out your vices as other people fulfill some happiness or accomplish their career goal. Your kindnesses, like your problems, are mere shallowness. You stand up for yourself through harassment, as if you were going to be swallowed whole. You beautiful, silly little girl. What nonsense they are, those words of yours. "My teddy bear, yes, my big tomcat . . . I like you very much, you know . . . Hold me close, closer, keep me warm . . . Freedom . . . I am your prisoner in freedom . . . I promise, I swear, at forty, you'll see, I shall be yours completely, my teddy bear . . . Don't give me that wild animal look, you frighten me . . . Oh, how you frighten me, my big, wild animal . . ."

Who are you really, you chameleon? You are the only one who can explain. You change your face all the time. You cry, you sing, you beg, you drag along behind me, you detest me, and then suddenly you roll yourself up inside the dignity of some small, sulking child, and you insist that I should feel ashamed of being at your feet.

It seems to me that there is something wonderfully perverse in your innocence. One telltale sign: your smile, which I love very much by the way, is perhaps only so beauti-

59

ful because it is superbly superficial, offered on the spur of the moment and only on the outside. Of course, you don't seem very anxious to associate it with those moments that presage the death of your childhood. That is why I would like to know the reasons which cause you to flee from your adult body as if you yourself were not its expert witness.

I don't think that I exaggerate your ambiguity. What I sense is that, in dealing with me, your fear of failing to disappoint me is less than your fear of cracking under your own inner tensions. You have faith in love, and that is precisely what blocks you and what provokes me. That I occasionally offer you something more than my desire in order to be accepted by you gets me nowhere. For you I am, and will unquestionably remain, a perverted bourgeois who can be attentive only to carnal pleasures. Of course, I would not give up those pleasures for anything in the world. Furthermore, they keep me sufficiently stable so that you and your whims can seduce me without having any scenes. But to reduce me to just that!

Often I wonder why I hang on, why you. I search for the crack. Very vague memories. Yes, of course one evening there were your eyes. I remember it well. I wondered then what it was that I should do to possess them. Not long afterwards, I began to dwell on your body: the different smiles you have, your false modesty, your breasts under taut fabric, a whole slew of little nothings that promised first to distract me, then to save me from my own torment. In front of one of your friends you dumbfounded me one fine evening at the Club Saint Hilaire by telling me that you refused to become a part of my life. As if I had asked you!

No, you see, I attach far too much importance to love to accept living with you day after day without the fear that your self-centeredness would ruin everything. Since you declare to everyone that love means nothing to you, I'd like for you to tell me some day, out loud, what those silences and those deep sighs of ours mean, then, since they only grow more profound as time goes on.

It is true that you see me as some sort of lavish entertainment. You are convinced that you must preserve the rules and regulations of your profession at any price, as well as the warped situation in which I find myself. I believe that to be the reason why you seem to refuse any reconciliation between what you are and what I feel towards you. Everything takes place as if I were forcing you, as if I were raping you. There are moments when I wish I really hated you, when I would like to hurt you. I imagine that my hatred, once let loose, will dissipate the resentment and bitterness of an ill-mannered street urchin that you tend to show me. Perhaps then you'll understand the advantages of your favored state.

It would be sufficient to give up on you, to turn my eyes away from you permanently, for you to notice that I belong to a noble breed. You forget one thing: very soon your loveliness will begin to wane; what seems normal to you now will cease to be so and will force you to yield to the facts.

Perhaps then you'll understand that your coyness toward me is nothing but a useless and idiotic game. Perhaps then, though, it will be too late. Bang, bang, bang. Finished. Curtains. Move over. Make a place for the young.

You should live fully today, right now. Why are you so eager to belong to those for whom suffering is a pleasure? Do you know that others in your place would grovel before me? So be stubborn and proud of it. What class! I believe that is the reason I persist in waiting for you. Partly out of compassion, partly out of laziness, and, I'd like to think, mostly out of goodness. Besides, a situation like this pleases me: in an unexpected way it converts the games of my political life —for now patiently on hold—into a reality. For me living today equals waiting, albeit by creating my own destruction. All love ought to lead to that. Is that too extreme? In any event, it is almost impossible for me to reverse my direction.

Points needing clarification:

—Last week, in Nairobi, I was a hair away from suicide. The conditions were perfect. What held me back was your little picture. Desire to survive or simply to see you again?

—It is true, as you said yesterday, that I am intolerably jealous. I really do want you to live your life as you see fit, but I am always afraid that you'll escape from me towards someone else. Is that fear not really an expression of insecurity: I don't know you, or rather more precisely, I don't know you very well!

—I would like for you to tell me in all honesty what

62

it is that ties you to me: friendship, affection, curiosity, or simply self-interest.

—I wonder: if you were to drop me some day, would I be capable of killing you out of spite? Sometimes you actually present me with the opportunity to humanize my ambitions. That undoubtedly is the root of the importance with which I have invested you.

II

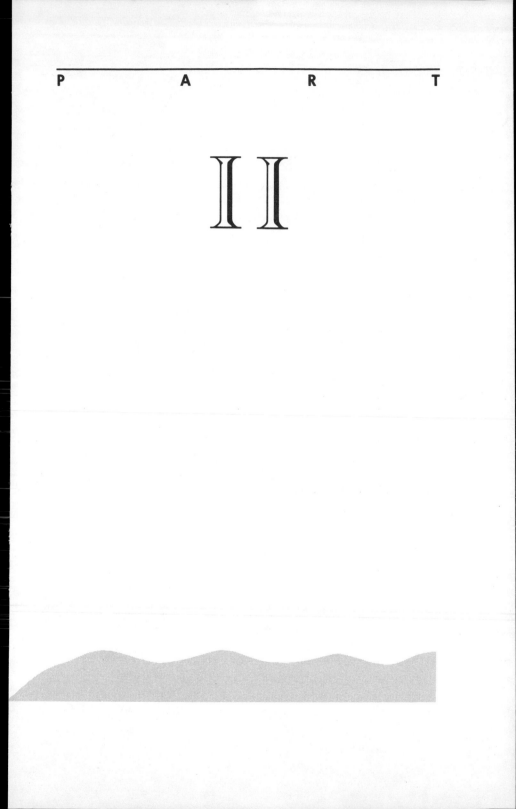

1

"We bring you greetings from Mulembe . . ."

This time they had been more casual: they had entered your little room without knocking, without even pretending to be police officials. They awakened you roughly, a few kicks in the lower back, gentle compared to the severe punishment of the previous day. There were still three of them, comfortable in their suits, silent, intimidating, serene. Deliberate monsters. They threw you on the floor. Both of you cried out, mostly out of fear, hoping without much confidence to attract the attention of possible passersby. They sat down on the bed, contemptuous of and completely ignoring your terrified female screams. In a low voice, the one who appeared to be the leader spat out:

"Shame of our tribe, we bring you both greetings from Mulembe. And to you, Ya, a last remembrance from your father. They've killed him. Some young people found his head near the Meli spring . . . His body disappeared . . . We never knew what they did to him . . ."

Your heart barely missed a beat. Your eyes opened roughly, windows exposed to a forgotten world: the green forests, the underbrush of wild ferns, the quiet waters full of fish, a savannah with gazelles, the plentiful fields surrounding a small, prosperous village: Mulembe . . . And your father the Chief, lord of another era, anachronistic old man, but wise and just. He was the incarnation of a past which, from your childhood on, seemed insignificant to you compared to the efficiency of the Whites . . . But you did love him, this simple little man, your father.

"He was a great man, a great chief, a great fighter. He died for the cause of his people . . ."

He was pacing back and forth, had found a bottle of Coca-Cola, had taken the cap off with his teeth, was drinking it straight from the bottle. Then he had gone to deposit it in the corner where you yourselves used to stack up the empty bottles. You were thinking of your father, dry-eyed, yourself astonished that you could not find a single tear to shed in mourning, if only for a brief moment. It was, instead, your girlfriend who was moaning, who was sniffling as discreetly as she was able. You approached her. Seeing her ravaged face, you dissolved in tears, finally heedful of the pain that ran through you. She had clutched your shoulders with her hands, then taken you close in her arms. Her warm hands on your back made you shiver. Huddled against her, your body had rediscovered hers: you were aware of her thighs as if frozen, now moist, ready to thaw out. "They killed him," you murmured; "He is dead, my father is dead . . ." Her belly against yours in that reminder of his death, you were shivering, bewildered, victim of a frenzy which your gasps and sobs kept going. Then you calmed down, afraid that they might guess what you were going through in their presence.

You had sat down on the floor to listen to what he had to say. He began by bringing your village back to life, then came back to your father.

"He died because he knew that things were not as they should be: there are the rich and the poor. The rich stand guard so that this difference will continue, so that there will always be the poor to be their slaves . . . In earlier days, in our villages, things were not like that . . . That is why we fought the Whites. They left . . . and now it is our own people, people of our own race, who . . ."

69

You were weeping quietly, your head on her shoulder. And breaks in your congested breathing betrayed moments of panic. In your grief, you were unconsciously using the occasion to relive those years of your youth as well, to be back in the place you came from. You were amazed that this land had become the object of the hypocritical games of money and trade, thus laying it open to outbursts of violence.

"Our men and our women still know the honor and the dignity of their past. That is why they struggle today for a little more justice; that is why they support the struggle of the liberation party . . . In the meantime, you two . . ."

You were growing less tense, scrutinizing him, you were beginning to understand through the blood and the stabbing pains of your battered body the deeper reasons for yesterday's punishment and this morning's brutality. A long time ago, your aged grandmother had taught you that one cannot wash one's face with just one finger. You were the fingers of a single hand, the limbs of a single body. You had forgotten him; they jostled you back, began again:

". . . Above all, Ya, you are not a child like any other. You are a descendant of the M'pfumu, of princes . . ."

Obviously. You were quite well aware that you had slid into another universe in order to survive. From your school years on, you had judged it right to cast aside the old aristocratic concepts of your class. A whole new world was out there waiting for you. Unbending nuns, the wives of God they said, dedicated to His worship and to His works, had taken you in hand. Having come from across the sea, these

70

virginal women had taught you that God was democratic and that the white people were bringing you Civilization, a great Civilization. Over the years, you had discovered the new exigencies of work thanks to them. Working was necessary, working to have money, money to live, to live according to the laws of the Lord in this world in order to deserve the afterlife... And above all, to know that the Faith, which together with the Holy Sacrament, would cause you gentle fits of despair, was a gift, a grace, which few enjoyed as you did.

Working for His glory... For the men there were construction sites; for the best among them there were medical schools or schools of agronomics. For a woman, for you, there was only marriage, the only possibility in what was a completely nonexistent future. The city had seduced you with its liberties: a strange upward mobility that had carried you to the sidewalks of Kinshasa and that, with the same stroke, had revealed to you that the good sisters were right, at least about one thing: work was a downfall, the consequence of original sin...

"Through your way of life," he was saying, "you are betraying us... Your people are suffering, are struggling for their freedom, and you two are not only finding pleasure in your bodies... But you, Ya, you are on the best of terms with the worst enemy of our tribe, the official girlfriend of an opponent to our cause..."

Both of you were sitting at their feet, having instinctively recovered the conventional way to be womanly. You

71

knew that he was right, that it was necessary to take part in the drama of your own people, without any uproar, to allow yourselves to be included.

"Continue your lives as you have before, but do it now for the common cause. Don't forget that we are at war: you are both fighters, in a particularly good position to find out what they are planning against us . . ."

He was breathing with difficulty, like a seriously stricken man. You were thinking that soon there would be another contact less for your people. You would have liked to cry out: "Go see a doctor, your life is needed by our people," but you knew that such an outcry was sacrilegious: the Ancestors were watching over him.

"Especially you, Ya, through your politician you can be of great help to us. If you think it's useful to live with him, do so; in that way you'll know every decision and every plan . . ."

"I've broken up with him," you countered timidly.

"A woman never breaks the attachment entirely, you know that. Be his slave, enter fully into his life or work with him."

"Yes, I will," you had answered in a small voice.

And again you had found the frenzy of a sacrament, that of a common origin, and at the same time the mystery of blood relationship. A new key to be inserted into your everyday habits. Your nights and your ecstasies in beds as yet unknown would answer from this moment on to the call of a major exploit. Finally, he laid down the rules:

72

"... A brother will come to look for you twice a week at the bar. The spacing of the meetings will vary. He knows you ... You'll tell him whatever you know ..."

He will come. An uncle or a cousin now in the business world. While he was there, they would play the intimidated girls or the beautiful flirts, convinced that this was one way in which to safeguard the ravaged landscape of their childhood.

"If by chance you should have an urgent message to get to us, go to the Great Market; there you will look for Ma Yene ... She sells vegetables ... Buy ome and ask her for news of her mother who has gone back o the village ... She will tell you that she's been waiting for r return for weeks ... Interrupt her twice, say that times are rd ..."

With small nods of their heads, the two young women indicated their agreement and unde ood that they were becoming knots in a large fishnet thro out to sea. They would walk the open road in front of th n, without questions, without problems either, ignorant o both the sources and the direction of the winds, and, if nee be, they would do so for the rest of their lives: the tribe req red no less.

"Never forget that you belong to a tribe of l ds. Remember your obligations. Like all your brothers and - ters, you may neither use nor touch any object that belongs a European: it is always tainted. If you should, purify yourselves according to the law. By the same token, in no way and under no circumstances will you eat the liver, heart, or head of any animal whatsoever. You know this and so it must be..."

The sun was coming in through the little window. In front of it billowed a large Dutch batik, a curtain bought on sale. The three men and the two women seemed at the same time sad and savage, reduced to nothingness in a suffering and a nameless hatred. They knew that they were to hurl themselves at the horns of mad animals, they each nurtured the same desire to survive the struggle, to be able to find their roots again afterwards: a communion in the same hope.

"Our enemies are Black like us... What we want is justice, equality, our independence. Our movement is open to members of other tribes who think as we do... But that is none of your business... In your assignment, never forget our people's rules: always be polite even with our enemies; never take anything that does not belong to you... If you borrow, never forget to return... No fight justifies meanness... Be careful also not to harm anyone... And, above all, know that from this moment on you are perhaps condemned to death, like so many of your brothers and sisters..."

2

It happened in the tritest possible way: I was sitting on the bed, overcome. She had dressed herself in silence in front of me, had taken her purse and her scarf and then, very calmly, in an artificial, throaty voice that I had never heard from her before:

"It's over now, Daddy. All over, forever."

Stunned, I was looking at her, feeling a little ridiculous, wondering what exactly it was that she was after.

"What's the matter now?"

"Only that it's over, my teddy bear. Finished, finished, finished . . . I am not interested in you. I'm leaving. You understand?"

She was gone, slamming the door. I thought I would wait for her return, telling myself that by then I would have pulled myself together. Everything would depend on what I'd be able to say to her. After an hour had passed, impatience won out and I left, convinced that it was quite possible she would return with the same face with which she had spoken her last words that morning. Better to leave and later on to send her a message, a word or two, and to wait.

My friend,

My very dear friend, you told me the day before yesterday that you no longer wish to see me: you are not interested in me. Faced with the choice you have imposed upon me, I wonder if I have permission to question myself on something other than myself. I have been forbidden to discuss your decision; I cannot even do so, for in such a discussion I could only rebel or accept. If I were to do the former, that amounts in the final analysis to a violation of you; and if the latter, to questioning, once again, the attitude I have had towards you since the beginning. All of these would contradict the principle of availability which I hold so dear. To dwell too long on the concrete implications of your decision would come down to the

76

same; at worst, it would mean trying to judge you by revealing the consequences of your decision.

After these two days, during which you seem to have systematically avoided me, I can at least afford the luxury of reflecting upon the circumstances of our breaking up. I would like to understand what happened, the how and the why, and that without passing judgement over you.

Even if I had sensed a crisis coming, I could have never imagined it would burst forth in such an unexpected way. Your coldness, last Friday, bothered me a little. Without convincing me, your explanations meanwhile did not portend a break. You might have prepared your departure a little better. But no, you had to treat me as if I were out of the picture; as if I had never been an equal partner in this relationship.

It took the humble courage of a slave, the following evening at the Club Saint Hilaire, to admit to you that I had no objection to your decision, and that I wished you good luck; and last night I actually asked your forgiveness for the harm that I may have done you. Humble courage, but what humiliation! I surprise myself.

I hold nothing against you. What right do I have to heap abuse upon you? Yet, I also know my own past: as you well know, I have had affairs. Sometimes to my distress, more often to my displeasure, I have been involved with women for whom I was the adored master. Never, though, to make my boredom clear to my partner, did I treat her as you did me. I admire the lashing disdain of the letter you sent me: "... Today

I have both the conviction and especially the strength to tell you that I must put an end to . . ." You say it well. And how I would like to get to know your conviction and your strength, just to understand!

In the wake of that, it staggers me that all you have found to be concerned about is my loneliness. What are you talking about, my poor friend? What loneliness? Be that as it may, I thought it quite splendid that your girlfriend came to your rescue this morning to apologize for your "moodiness," as she put it. She was jubilant and I am still wondering about the reasons for her excitement. On the whole, she is a very bad actress. In my desire to ignore my jealousy, I settled for hearing her out and answering her as it seemed she wanted to be answered.

I have only one question left: I want to know if I was wrong when, from the onset, I suspected that your feelings towards me came under the heading of a form of egotism.

According to your friend, you are asking yourself a different question: to know how to behave with men. She offered me the juicy and frankly quite sickening stories of your disasters with men. As far as I know, nobody has ever taken you by force. What is so abnormal, then, in men noticing you when you provoke them? On that very point, remember what you classified as a stinging remark only a short while ago: "Little one, it does pay off to be an always available institution." Your decision to leave me has certainly neither weakened nor confirmed that remark, but, on the other hand, has it not hardened the walls of your self-centeredness? That you are saturated with, disgusted by males could always encourage you to

*change your life and your profession; it doesn't have to make
you refuse love itself. Since then I've been trying to figure out
to what truth you are sacrificing me.*

*It would not surprise me if your "big decision" to break
up with me had been influenced by the murky friendship you have
with this girl who plays at being a profligate. I believe that she is
totally capable of manipulating you. Remember, if you will, my
questions about you two. This morning she appeared in person to
see me: obviously jealous of the feelings you had for me, calculat-
ing, narrow-minded, and pretentious, above all.*

*Finally, I wanted to tell you that I fervently wish you
to go all the way with your choice. I have never imposed
anything upon you; why should I now seek to do so? I am only
trying to understand your choice. Do me some justice, then, by
recognizing the fact that up to this very day, I have, at every
turn, wanted to guess at and be ahead of your wishes. After the
breakup of what you so ludicrously call 'preferential love,' I do
not understand why you would want to hand me the alms of a
"friendship." No, be rational, and keep your friendship for
other people . . ."*

He was feeling very much at ease in the somber atmosphere of the bar. Comfortably settled in his armchair, with
an inattentive gaze, he was observing the infinitely sweet
warmth which, with the alcohol, was making its way through
his body. He decided that the lights were shifting because of
the music's shift to a jazz piece. With one ear he was listening
to his friend, the attorney, who would not stop talking. A

crazy hope was working away at him: if, as rumor had it, he would once again be Minister of State, would she come back to him? He felt a wave of tenderness invade him, flow soft and thick into his eyes. The girls were beautiful, lovely as goddesses. How beautiful Black is, he said to himself. His eyes roamed from the two European women, leaning on the counter, to the African ones, who were dancing. He preferred to rest his eyes on the latter. He was intrigued by a young couple. He tried to follow what the orchestra was playing:

> *Well, Crocodile Rockin' is something shockin'*
> *When your feet just can't keep still*
> *I never knew me a better time*
> *An' guess I never will . . .*

The music embedded itself in his flesh, intermingled with his blood. He was happy and began to smile, surprised to see a motionless barmaid sitting at the far end of the counter, lost in thought, her head at a slight angle resting on the flat of her left hand. A lovely gazelle at rest, herself indifferent to all grace and beauty. He sipped his drink, dreaming of nude young girls dancing in circles in a field of blooming canna. He felt singled out by the gods, because the president of his Party had told him that the Party had pinned all its hopes on him for the government now to be formed. Once again, they were promising to shower him with honors. The lawyer persisted in talking:

"Do you believe in witchcraft?... No? Neither do I. However, as far as I'm concerned, I must clarify that I sometimes wonder whether witchcraft is not basically, well, whether it isn't really something different from what it is generally thought to be... Look here..."

The lawyer grabbed his arm and carried him along in his complicated tale. For a moment, and in full agreement, he followed his words, then gave up to continue his daydreaming. He was remembering his own reaction to the President's proposals:

"You do me great honor, Sir. I thank you for the confidence you have in me... Yes, Sir... I did have lunch with the President of the Assembly... No, it was not yet mentioned there. I believe that he wanted to sound me out ... The Department of Foreign Affairs? Do you think that would be a possibility?... Yes, certainly... It is entirely up to you to see... If that doesn't work out, we could fall back on the Department of Finance or Economics... Agreed... Yes... Absolutely..."

He was optimistic. The afternoon's telephone calls had strengthened his hopes. Early in the evening, at the "Colibri," he had run into the President-to-be of the Council. The conditions offered seemed normal enough to him: he was to deposit a million francs in a Swiss bank account as soon as he took office. Very smoothly, everything was being set in operation. A tall, slender waitress with the face of one of the Madonna's children came to freshen their drinks. As she bent down, some locks of hair from her wig brushed against his face. His nostrils quivered as he inhaled a strong scent of patchouli. With shining eyes, she offered him an apologetic smile and left. His fingers slid off the armrest. He began to tap the leather in time with the song.

But they'll never kill the thrills we got
Burning up to the Crocodile Rock
Learning fast as the weeks went past,
We really thought the Crocodile Rock would last.

The lawyer let loose. "Did you see her? You did, didn't you? You know what's going on? She wants you to go with her. No reaction? All these whores, they make me sick. If that's civilization . . . This would simply be unthinkable in the village . . ." He was bent on letting the afternoon move on by, he thought of himself as heir to the heavens and master of these lovely bodies drenched in perfume and sweat, coming and going. The lawyer had made up his mind.

"So that's it, this civilization of yours? Is this what you call civilization?"

"Come on, friend, are you kidding, or what? Is this really the first time you've been here?"

His laughter was icy. He seemed taken aback by the violence of the response. He remained silent.

"What do you want me to do? She earns her living as she can."

Incredulous, the attorney shook his head. His eyes

narrowed to the point where they became two tiny, tapered horizontal lines.

"You have been a statesman. You may well be one again soon . . . And you find it appropriate to defend this sort of imported debauchery . . . That is what capitalism is, or at least one of its essential aspects: moral corruption . . ."

"You really believe that?"

"What? You don't believe it? Go to China . . . Closer yet, in your own village, are there places like this, are there girls like this? This dissipation and licentiousness that invades us from abroad . . ."

"And it pleases us, doesn't it? We are here, aren't we, you and I, drinking, carried away by our desire to live life to the fullest, hoping that two naked girls, built like our waitress, will kneel down in front of us, right there, each of them with a basket of fruit, sweets in one hand and a tray with glasses of champagne in the other."

"But that's . . . that's depraved!"

Disconcerted, he straightened up in his seat just a little. Depraved? He felt as if he were in the center of perfect harmony, did not understand that such quiet order could not be responded to with the complete freedom to live out all one's dreams. He was breathing regularly, the breath of his blood, the breath of the masters of the universe. With a motion of his hand, he ordered a new round of drinks and closed his eyes, hoping to float on a lake, like a bouquet of roses offered to the spirits of the sun and the rain. He murmured: "But in depravity lies hope." The orchestra bore him out:

> *. . . Oh, teacher, I need you*
> *Like a little child*
> *You got something in you*
> *To drive a schoolboy wild . . .*

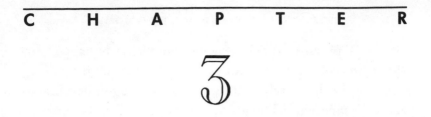
ossession had taken hold. It was the only thing real in this penthouse where passions in heat and blended perfumes mingled and interchanged with perspiration of all kinds, the stale smells of alcohol, and the smoke of cigarettes and cigars. A whole world ablaze, drunk with music, raw nerves, careening down a steep slope.

A prisoner of this general complicity, he tapped out the rhythm of the dance with both hands. Was he still playing a part or was he merely waiting for his cunning to lead him to a state of innocence? Intrigued, the lawyer was watching him. He was taken by surprise.

"Go ahead, my dear counselor, you think I'm quite lit, don't you? Don't deny it, my friend, tell me whether my breath really smells of liquor . . ."

They laughed out loud. He knew that throughout this night he'd abhor feeling any regrets. Yet, he said to himself, I must have some weapon so as not to overstep the bounds. Yes, a weapon. It appeared of its own accord: he would make him talk in order to disengage himself from the man's verbiage, to daydream on, and to drink less. The lawyer loves to talk. If need be, he will oversaturate him.

"Drinking, indeed! My uncle on my father's side really knew how to drink. In the village, he could drink for two days straight. On the third day, he would bring us together, my brothers and myself, so that he could hold forth on the martial feats of our people and lecture us for the entire afternoon . . . The white man's civilization brought us that, as you said . . . but it caused us to forget how to experience joy directly."

"It brought us that and other things, too, like insane asylums, old-age homes, and orphanages. But it's that, above all, that . . . that . . ."

"That bothers you? What a true legalist you are. That's what life is all about, though, my friend."

86

"No."

"Oh, come now! Why do we kill ourselves working if it isn't for that? Women, women, women, women . . . and fame . . . What do you work for, then?"

"What if I told you that I work just to live?"

"Yes, to live. Well-being and pleasure. Find me something else that makes more sense . . . If you want we can choose some lovely slave girls. They'd dance for us, right here in front of everyone, with wreaths of petunias or bougainvillea around their necks as their only decoration . . ."

"You really are depraved!"

"Any more so than lawyers are? I simply enjoy the privileges of the noble and am happy to do so. The music and the girls are beautiful this evening, so let's indulge our desires. Unless, of course, you want us to take two slave girls along right this minute . . ."

"No, I prefer not to have anything to do with the orgies of you politicians . . ."

"That's because politics is the domain of kings. It permits such liberties! Have you noticed the ways of popular politicians?"

The attorney did not answer. He shrugged his shoulders. It seemed unlikely to him that the other had spoken in complete earnest. He was either repressed or a shameful old lecher, this lawyer, he thought. More than ever, the overall atmosphere in the bar was that of a wild celebration of the encounter of gigantic ground swells born of luxuriant profusions and scents from all over the world. He felt in fine

87

shape, knowing that the night, as usual, was anointing him. He wanted to know, at all costs.

"I didn't know you were still practicing the terror of the cathechism, my dear friend. Bless me, Father, for I have sinned and I do not repent . . ."

"Must you blaspheme?" the lawyer retorted.

"No, I was just kidding. I'm stirring up your apathy. You seem a little drunk to me."

"No, my friend, I am sad."

Taken aback, he scratched his neck, waiting for what was to follow. Crystal-clear peals of laughter from the next table saved him: they made him think of the wide-open, golden hearts of the daisies in his yard. Gentle now, he turned back to the lawyer. He seemed completely drunk: a nasty, disheveled face with heavy bags under bloodshot eyes. He felt sorry for him, took his arm.

"Why get depressed?"

"I had wanted to be a priest, you know. They threw me out of the seminary. I don't know what I'm looking for . . ."

"Earn your living. Make yourself a bundle, more each day . . . You'll have power and make people happy . . . You'll see . . ."

"Well, maybe. I no longer want anything other than that . . . You know, my father is an alcoholic. I hate him. He is always after me. Always wants money . . . always . . . There are more than twenty of them at my house right now, waiting for me to come home . . . waiting for the bank notes I hand out every day . . . Uncles, aunts, cousins, pigs, swine . . . You see what I mean?"

"I see, yes. It's the same with me."

"That's why I'm here."

Two tears began to run down his face, whitish pearls against a gloomy background. He clasped his arm, said gently:

"So, all the more reason to really try to forget. In gratuitous pleasure. Here and elsewhere, freely. You must understand that what would be really depraved is to live as a prisoner of those swine, as you just said . . ."

Lights were falling in multicolored ribbons. The orchestra was oozing a slow number. Clear, syncopated notes, fleshed out, gushing forth like a waterfall. He began again, more gently still:

"Do you remember our games as young university students once we discovered the fruits which the good fathers were hiding from us? The *Songs of Bilitis* by Pierre Louys? Do you remember?"

He recited:

. . . *Forest shadow, where she was to be, tell me: where has my mistress gone?—She went down to the plain.—Plain, where has my mistress gone?—She followed the river's edge— Rolling river, who has seen her pass, tell me, is she nearby?— She has left me for the wooded path.—Path, do you see her still?—She has left me for the open road.*

89

BEFORE THE BIRTH OF THE MOON

His eyes clouded, his voice hoarse, trembling with emotion, the lawyer joined in as the orchestra was being applauded:

Oh, white road, city road, tell me where have you led her?—To the golden street that leads to Sardis.—Oh, street of light, are you touching her naked feet?—She has entered the king's palace. Oh, palace, splendor of the earth, give her back to me!—Look, she wears necklaces on her breasts and baubles in her hair, one hundred pearls down along her legs, two arms around her waist."

The waitress, bewildered, was watching them, tray in hand. With a snap of his fingers he broke the magic.

"Another round, please. But with two extra glasses. And tell the two ladies with nothing else to do, there at the counter, that I'm inviting them to join us. If you'd like to do the same after your shift is over, you will not be sorry."

They came over: two young, dazzling animals, tall and slender, delicate, with the eyes of does. They sat down across from them, pretending in the movements of their hands and necks to be women of the world. The attorney recovered his strength. He asked him:

"Tell me some more about witchcraft."

"It has rather more to do with the question of the absurdity of the law in the matter. Is that all right with you?"

"Fine."

"The other day in court, someone accused his brother-in-law of practicing witchcraft. It seems that the brother-in-law eats children. Two kids supposedly have already died in his house of some mysterious illness. Tell me what the judicial opinion was."

"No; really, I know nothing about these things; nothing at all."

"Well, listen carefully: the false accusation of witchcraft brought about compensation for the accused and punitive sanctions."

"How come?"

"This is the way it works: since witchcraft doesn't exist, an accusation of this sort can only come under the heading of libel."

The lawyer burst out laughing. He leaned back in his armchair that creaked slightly.

"And how about this one, my dear man: a defendant accuses the wife of the plaintiff of having bewitched him and of having caused an incurable illness. Judgement?"

"Accusation founded on insubstantial evidence."

"Excellent. You're making progress, you see. But let's suppose that at the house of the plaintiff's wife a horn is found, filled with strange items, carefully hidden behind the kitchen utensils. And furthermore, that it is her father who accuses her of being a witch . . ."

It was exactly two thirty-five when he saw her. She must have entered very discreetly. He had not seen her come in. While the lawyer was explaining the problem to him, he was watching her dreamily. Her companion seemed young, extremely young even. He could only see him from the back. The neck of a bull in his prime. The shoulders of a boxer.

Where did he come from? He had never met him. And yet, he thought he knew all the friends of his former mistress. She was laughing, her head thrown back, showing her bare throat. Had she seen him? She was completely herself, adorable, dressed in a bush shirt. He had never liked those on other women: rough and ugly cotton or unbleached linen, big military pockets creased by the leather belt. She made it look softer, made it more womanly, with small plackets under the arm, wide flowing loops which, keeping her belt in place, made her upper body look slim and long, accentuated by her white pants.

He took off his jacket to make himself more comfortable. The lawyer was talking to the girls about rainmakers. He paid no attention to him so that he could take better notice of the immense jealousy settling inside him.

They were dancing now: two frantic shadows. Her white pants reflected the bluish lights. As he watched them, he remembered the ardor of first communion. A feeling of powerlessness. She had surrendered, her head on his shoulder. He was picturing her languid lips brushing against his neck, as if by chance. For a few seconds the mirror set onto one of the pillars, reflected her face back to him: her eyes were closed, her false eyelashes calmly resting; her slightly open mouth showed the shimmer of her teeth. A woman entranced. The slow dance linked them closely. She was hardly moving her hips. Her arms, two lengths of cloth around a neck. The dark fruits of her chest must be crushing against the man. He felt rage rise to his head in a hot and

92

violent rush. He got up. The lawyer tried to hold him back:

"No, what are you doing? You're not leaving me by myself like this. And with two girls on my hands . . ."

He calmly put on his jacket, buttoned it, reached into his pants pocket with his left hand, pulled out wads of large bills and threw them on the table.

"Ladies, I entrust my friend to you . . . You're going to take good care of him and do everything to make him happy. Help yourselves. I'll see you again one of these nights!"

He went out, tall, head held high, both hands in his pockets, escorted by a melody that wrenched his stomach.

Saw your hands trembling, your eyes opened in surprise
It's ninety in the shade, babe, and there ain't a cloud in the sky.
I called you my child, said honey, now this is our game,
There's two of us to play it and I'm happy to be home again.

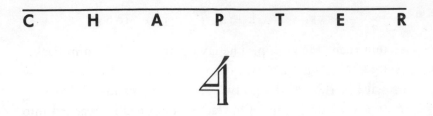

4

e had awakened with a troubled mind, the idea in his head that some urgent task needed attention. He searched through the fog of the previous day's events, got lost in the whirlwind of last night's reception. They had celebrated his appointment as Minister. Once again. Friends, relatives had come in large numbers to congratulate him. The President of his Party appeared in his thoughts, then disappeared again. No, it wasn't he. She, too, had come, unobtrusive as always, with her protectress friend by her side. She was laughing heartily: ". . . Why do you look at me like that? It's very simple, isn't it? I'm here to offer my congratulations to the hero of my dreams . . ."

There had been a small scuffle. He remained preoccupied. Some compelling task. He had merged with the pain encircling his head. He got up, felt the weight of his body. I should lose some pounds, he thought, I'm gaining too much. Then it came to him. Undone, he made a sign of distress with his head. "The thrill of honors and of the carnal." It was she who had whispered this to him as she was leaving. At that very moment, he had expressed his thanks although he was puzzled: he thought he had heard "honors and cattle." It wasn't until later, yes, until his Master arrived and reminded him of his duty to sacrifice, that he had understood the mockery.

At his Master's very first words he had frowned: "Some goats or a young girl." He was feeling his anger mount, was smiling as if it concerned only an innocuous social event. He was sipping his champagne, listening to the Master with one ear, the other attentive to the sounds and the movements in the room, his eyes darting around his newly decorated living room. He was the center of gaiety, of the party's commotion, the flowers, lights, and paintings everywhere in this huge, official house. He was king, a king with the face of a good child, placid, full of the warmth of friendship; at the same time, he was trying to discover wiles and hidden implications in the eyes of those with whom he was talking, or underneath their words. In the living room and the garden, shimmering men's shirts, long *pagne*-dresses in vivid colors, women mostly young and beautiful, men in evening clothes, relaxed, looking happy. The thrill had arrived, blissful and sweet.

It was when he passed the glass door which led to the kitchen that he woke up completely and remembered the conversation with his Master. He stood still for a moment. Yes, that was it. The standing lamp next to which they found themselves strangely altered the Master's face: he had a swarthy skin tone and greenish eyes; his eyelids looked as if they were made of leather. He persisted:

"You know that you must protect yourself against the envious. Do you really think that all your guests tonight are friends of yours? We will welcome you into our Society, if you so desire."

"But I already belong."

"Oh, no, my son. That was just a first stage."

"What are the conditions? And how much is it going to cost me this time?"

Slightly drunk, he was feeling borne on high by the gods and was astonished that he might need to take precautions. With an authoritative smile, he tried to read the Master's face with its hard features. It was impassive, the mouth slightly twisted. His pronounced squint gave him a frightful expression. At least, he was lucky, he thought, that the Master had agreed to come dressed in suit and tie. Had he arrived decked out in the costume of the Order . . . He would have been the talk of the town the next morning. Yes, he felt grateful towards him for that above all else.

"To join the Society permanently, you must offer a victim as do all novices: a young girl or, as a substitute sacrifice, ten goats. And to consecrate the initiation that will make you one of us completely, it is, instead, a man or ten oxen that must be sacrificed, according to time-honored custom."

Helped by the wine, he found the proposal astounding. A couple was coming towards him. With a step to the left, he approached them . . . "Good evening, Madame . . . Sir, thank you for coming . . . —But, Your Excellency, the honor is ours entirely . . . Yes, indeed, we'll be in touch soon. —Let me hear from you whenever, at your convenience . . ." He had begun to play with the champagne glass.

"Yes, agreed, I'll make the arrangements, Master."

"When?"

"Tomorrow or the day after. You can see that I really must spend a little time talking with everyone here tonight . . ."

"No, my son. The proverb says: "Water has sprung from the breast of the stone, give praise to God and protect the rock: it will herald marvelous things." You must indicate your sacrificial victim to me immediately. Thus, we will be able to celebrate the sun and the harvesting season tomorrow evening."

"Fine. That is a good reason. I would gladly offer goats. But you're saying that you prefer a young girl?"

"It is the preference of tradition."

All by itself, a face etched itself in his mind. To separate them at last. A flash of lightning: once her guardian was gone, she would see the extent of the power and the will of the gods.

"Take that young woman . . . The tall one in white who looks as if she's protecting the girl I just kissed . . . Yes, that one; I offer her to you: she is not of my family, she is an enemy of mine."

She was laughing heartily, her head bent lightly backwards, her throat and chest heaving with pleasure and life.

He lingered in front of the mirror to erase the imprint of the night before, entertained himself with the bubbles he was able to create, for no reason at all, by blowing between his fingers. Still in his pajamas, he went into the pantry to have his breakfast. His wife, a heavy, sweet, matronly woman, was waiting for him. She sat down placidly across from him. A serviceable tool, she handed him what he needed with great economy of motion: coffee and cream, slices of bread, butter, jam, cheese, ham, cake . . .

Absentmindedly, he turned the radio on. They were replaying the speech delivered by the Chief of State the night before.

... Let us never forget that those who hold a public mandate are the target of all the people. It is upon the discipline which you will impose upon yourselves, upon the example which you will set, that the prestige of the Nation and the authority of the State depend. It is difficult to require our population to submit to the law if those who make the law are the first to trample it under their feet. Is not the legislator himself the first servant of the law that he imposes upon all others? And is not his most pressing duty to have respect for the law? In the exercise of your duties, gentlemen, public opinion is particularly observant of your behavior. No matter how serious a debate may be, it is important that it remain courteous and continue to observe the proprieties. Each and every one of you has the right to expect his colleagues . . .

"Are you really listening to this morality lesson?"

She spoke softly. He looked at her, thought that a quiescent cow would be no different at all. He saw the clash coming, preferred to avoid it.

"No, darling, turn it off."

She turned the button, gave him another cup of coffee with cream. With a wavering finger, he skimmed the hot liquid as he added a cube of sugar.

"When you have time," she began again, "will you

consider making an appointment with the surgeon at the University Hospital for the boy's circumcision . . ."

"A surgeon? But any general practitioner can do that. We have no lack of hospitals or dispensaries in the neighborhood. As far as I'm concerned, I'd have more faith in nurses."

"Butchers. Have you ever seen them work?"

"Come, come, darling, don't exaggerate. In any event, they're less expensive."

"As far as that goes, yes. Less expensive . . ."

Surprised by the cutting edge in her voice, he raised his eyebrows. He saw the rage grow in her eyes: her face became tense, the veins suddenly stood out on her forehead. But her voice was amazingly calm when she derided him with:

"And what about your mistresses, are they less expensive?"

"Listen, dear . . ."

"No, leave me alone."

He got up, was gone long enough to get dressed, then went downstairs. The official car, a black Mercedes, had pulled up, its door open. He settled himself in the back, mumbling "radio." Again he heard the voice of the President of the Republic:

. . . The enforcement of majority rule can prove to be very critical. Questions that implicate regional interests can sometimes require that solutions be

100

found, issued not by a majority but by general consent. An opinion may be considered a minority opinion, but not if it concerns a population whose regional interests are at stake. General consent is, furthermore, a truly African solution, as we confront problems which are, in turn, also particular to the Africa of today. On the eve of the second legislature . . ."

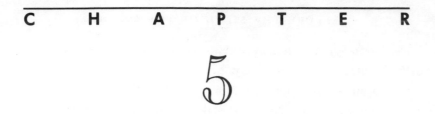

dream? An interminable tunnel. Darkness. He was watching himself live. Six o'clock. When he left his office, the rays of the setting sun, soothing flashes, were playing on the trees and the tin rooftops. A humid heat persisted despite a western wind. He disappeared into the car, had the air conditioning turned on. The car started. An extended dream?

Throughout the day, despite an enormous amount of work, many appointments, and some fooling around with his secretary behind his locked office door, he had not managed to drive from his mind the horror of a drunken gesture. Now it was undoubtedly a little late. In his Mercedes, lovely black blade of metal, he was sped along over the buckled asphalt of the road, in certain places even quite warped, on the outskirts of Kinshasa. He let himself be enveloped by his own madness. He no longer feared his bad conscience of the morning and felt that his own arguments throughout the day held a certain truth. Whoever it might be, was it not best to offer an enemy in consecration of the patience of the earth and the wishes of the Ancestors? The Master had told him the evening before that it was through such sacrifices that our Tradition makes its resources fruitful.

Night had fallen when they left the suburbs. The driver took a dirt road, drove for about ten minutes with all lights on high, then stopped the car in front of an isolated hut. The headlights closed in upon the old man. He was seated right on the ground, somewhat stooped, a pipe in his mouth. The flaps of his robe were fluttering. He saw him get up with difficulty, make a slight sign of greeting with his right hand. He gave his orders to the driver and went to meet the Master. In a sort of trance, he heard the car back up and leave. The Master was speaking:

"All is ready, my son, you have done well to come. You know the truth of the Ancestors: "The sun does not wish to be celebrated while it is living... Come and let us pray before the birth of the moon."

They walked around the hut. A tom-tom resounded in the distance. The west wind was blowing, bringing with it diffuse sounds from the forest. He was groping his way forward, both apprehensive and excited. When they stopped they were in a clearing. He sensed the presence of those initiated to the highest rank. He tried to make them out, vague shadows seated in a circle, legs crossed, hands on their knees, undoubtedly according to custom. He saw the Master sit down, and it was at that moment that he noticed a form whose hands and feet were bound together, lying flat on the ground in front of the Master. He recoiled slightly.

"Come forward," the Master told him. "Come forward so that the Ancestors may consecrate and protect you forevermore. Come forward and stand up, to the right, even with the head of this sacrifice which we will offer together to our Ancestors..."

The group repeated the call in chorus. With hesitant feet he took two steps, his thoughts a jumble of confusion, but he ended up by taking his place while the group repeated the call a third time. Believe, he thought, in the unity of their hearts. This sacrifice is part of the normal ritual. Nevertheless, he felt ill at ease; he hoped for a moment that something unexpected might occur to save the young woman's life. In the end, the promise of the gods swept him away and a smile came to his lips: The taste of hope, he said to himself. Here lies my strength against the enemies of my own people, against the envious and the jealous. To divert his attention, he called to mind the catechism and the religious lessons: the truth of another spiritual universe that precludes neither massacres nor murders on a grand scale, sometimes for the world balance of power, often for the possession and accumulation of great wealth. He heard that he was being called.

"There is nothing in the heavens," the Master was reciting, "nothing in the waters, nothing on earth, nothing beneath the soil, that does not belong to You. You are the salvation of our children, the accomplishment of your sons, Master of Life, your death is the presence which takes on our torment; your glory is the forgiveness for our unfaithfulness to the Law. Master of the Waters, watch over your descendant who stands here before you . . ."

The voice anchored itself in his consciousness, was penetrating his body. A shiver shook him. Almost despite himself, he adhered to the monotonous voice that quavered into the night. He looked for the Master's face, then realized that he was dreaming: in turn, each person present took up the ritual formula:

"According to the rules of the World and by the grace of God, through which You reign, what brings us together here in the dusk is Your goodness towards Your descendants. Protect them, Living Suns of the universe; protect them from ill health, from suffering, from godlessness. All that which emanates from You can only direct us to order and to the measure of Your Faith. Above all, bless our son here with us, chosen among the few, chosen from the masses, bless him and enfold him . . ."

The palms of his hands were growing icy. Tense, he began to wonder whether he was going to have to recite this prayer, forced himself in vain to remember its phrases, then gave up. The effort condensed the anguish inside his mouth: he felt very, very small, a little child caught making a mistake, now to make a fool of himself in front of all the members of the Society. In despair, his hands tightly grasped the edge of his jacket, when he heard the Master take up the long litany again.

"There is nothing in the heavens . . ."

The moon had risen. The shades of the initiated had materialized, fat, squat logs, with human heads amid the monolithic shafts of the forest arcade. Upright, with crossed arms, the Master intoned the ancestral litany. The hours of days gone by, of all the centuries past, flowed through the gasping utterances of the priest, violent torrents in an uproar of the late season's tremendous rain. The priest stopped suddenly; in a small voice, he summoned him:

"My son, come and meet your own people. May they enfold you now and forevermore."

He found himself on his knees, next to the young woman. He could feel a light, tepid breath on his calves. He directed his attention to the Master who was reciting the formula of the Sacrifice. He heard an assistant light the fire

106

behind his back and, at the same time, saw the white knife flat in the hands of the priest. It shone in the moonlight. Another assistant, a little old man, all bones and silver hair, came to sit down at the victim's left side; as he chanted, he put his hands over her eyes and her mouth and stretched her throat forward. The young woman let them do as they pleased, either possessed by the atmosphere of the mystery which she beheld, or completely submissive because she had been drugged. Holding it firmly by its handle, the priest raised the knife towards the sky. The sacred hymn burst forth. All those present sang in chorus:

Fafa Kandi, emi bona oke Kieze;
Obikakiila we nd'oto nda lobiko loke nd'okili bone
Eki we obwe njokokundaka
o bolotsi mongong' okela' inndiwa y'ikulaka
Emi la jiotsi likam liuma tolanga otobatela,
otosakele bokako ko osa
kele bokakonda belemo ekam.
Onsoko ja belotsi beuma
nel'eko otokaa ekemo.*

*Translation: Father Kandi, my Father, I am your son Kieze; I have always lived according to your laws while you were with me on this earth. After your death, I have fulfilled my duties and I have guarded over your burial. My people and I, myself, hope for your protection, your blessing upon all that we do. Shower us with your benefits, material and spiritual both; protect my people.

An attendant placed the victim back on the ground. Other formulas followed the hymns. He was now standing, facing the low flames, motionless, watching the smoke as it rose and got lost in the air. The victim was peacefully stretched out, her mouth slightly open, eyes closed. She had become a silent wall, providing protection against all his nightmares yet to come, against all eventual troubles and intrigues. He felt like laughing: his nerves were beginning to relax. He recalled the visit she had paid him. She was wearing a little grey suit that looked wonderful on her. Her shoes, with heels far too high, made her seem taller than she really was. From the outset, she had taken to looking him deep in the eyes in silence, which had intimidated him.

"I am truly very sorry," she had told him. "Sometimes my sister is hard to fathom. She says that she no longer sees anything in your relationship. Just a whim, I'm sure . . ."

"Yes," he had answered, annoyed.

"Let's hope that it will blow over . . . Perhaps it would be better to leave her alone for a few weeks. Wait until she makes a move . . ."

"But I love her!"

"So she told me. Undoubtedly, that is at the root of her problems. Do you really attach that much importance to that feeling? With all that you have . . . your power, your wealth . . ."

She was holding one hand flat on her abdomen, without any self-consciousness. He had wondered whether she had intestinal problems.

"Unfortunately for you, my dear, I attach a great deal of importance to this. At the present time everything leads me back to this love, you understand? I would marry her if she so desired."

"Yes," she had murmured feebly, as if shattered.

"It's true. I can see the difficulties I would face were I to do it. She is not of the same tribe . . . not to mention her profession . . ."

"That's just it, you tell her that too often. She's all upset because of that. Let her come around by herself. You are crushing her . . ."

Her voice had become a hiss. Her eyes were shining, the fingers of her left hand were absentmindedly stroking the edges of her jacket. With her right hand she was tapping the armrest of her chair. Calmly she continued:

"Perhaps she does not love you at all. Give her some time to figure it out."

"Listen . . . You are insinuating . . ."

"Please, Sir, I beg of you, don't get upset. I am simply trying to help a friend. You love her. She is my sister as well . . . We do come from the same tribe . . . She is so very young, so difficult, you know that . . ."

"I understand her problems, but what about you?"

"You know, she has never had any luck with men . . ."

~

Sitting in the hut, across from the Master, he was holding her liver in his hands. The fire had shriveled it. He no longer thought of it as a living part of that body which had defied him. His face no longer showed anything other than cold strength, an aggressiveness that was calm by nature: the traits of the kingdom of the initiated. He knew himself to have become a hurricane, a whirlpool in the heart of a river against which no floodgate could hold. From now on, no one but a fool would dare touch him. His only concern would be to avoid giving his own people occasion to condemn an offense against the Law or against God committed on his behalf.

After the communion, while the priest was giving thanks to the Ancestors, he inhaled, contented, the living air of those who had come from the hereafter. Once the prayers were brought to an end, the Master came before him, invited him to stand, clasped him in his arms and said in his deep voice:

"The sacrifice has been offered according to the ancestral wishes and the rites. Go in peace, my son, and may our Ancestors protect you and may they see that we go with you. Go in peace, my son."

A final embarkment, he thought. He was happy. He wanted to express his gratitude, did not know what to say, mumbled:

"Thank you . . . Thank you very much . . . Tomorrow, before evening falls, I will give the price of twenty oxen to the Society."

Barely having said this, he thought his proposal improper and the figure laughable. The Master looked him straight in the eyes, patient and imperturbable. As if to apologize, he added, in confusion:

"A first token of my gratitude . . ."

In vain he tried to open his eyes. To see the light, to wake up, he thought.

III

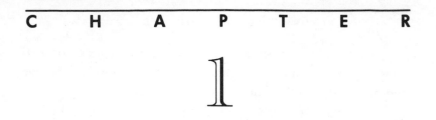

C H A P T E R

1

He had received you at last, around ten o'clock, after having kept you waiting for over an hour. You were quite sure that he had done it on purpose. But you were barely in his presence when your anger had disappeared by itself, and anguish had risen in your throat again; you had burst into tears:

"My friend, she's gone . . . She's been gone for two days . . . She doesn't come home, she doesn't come to the bar anymore . . . Help me, please . . ."

With a fatherly gesture, he had taken you by the shoulders. Moving away from his enormous desk, he had led you to a sitting corner whose walls were upholstered in beige, he had made you sit down in a deep easy chair with pillows covered in leatherette; he had pressed a button to start the air conditioner, had turned on the lights that were installed in the walls, and had sat down across from you in a rocking chair. You could feel him watching you, a male aware of his power, a minister of state convinced of his importance and of his might. He was analyzing you, insignificant little thing. You lowered your face, mute with shame, desperate. If he wanted to take revenge, you thought, he wouldn't act any differently.

"You're the only one who can help me, help me to find her again . . ."

"Go to the police."

"You knew very well the police can't do anything . . . They'll do nothing for me . . ."

"For you or for her?"

His tone was dry. Your tearful look met the eyes of a sated lion. He was mocking you, certain that he was in command. Torn between astonishment and humiliation, you thought nevertheless that you might soften him.

"She's my sister. You know that . . ."

"Why don't you go and see the politicians of your own tribe? There are certainly enough of them . . . You play with

116

me, with my feelings . . . and then, when you're in trouble, all of a sudden I am the only one who can . . ."

The intercom buzzed. He left his armchair to sit on the corner of a sofa set in an alcove. With a rough gesture, he touched a button on a machine sunk into a mahogany shelf. Your eyes on the ceiling, brokenhearted, tense, you were following the conversation.

"Your Excellency, in four minutes you will be receiving the Secretary General of the Department of Foreign Trade, in twenty minutes the Ambassador of . . ."

You could sense it: to see what effect his schedule had on you, he was watching your face as it cracked into the many little pieces of a puzzle.

"Allow me to remind you also," the secretary's voice continued, "that you have to chair a meeting of the interministerial group for African Cooperation at the end of the afternoon. The Chairman of the Cabinet insists on being seen immediately after the Ambassador; he would like to submit the dossier . . ."

Instinctively, you had picked up your purse knowing that he would not have another moment to spare for you, and you wondered how you could possibly think of pulling him back into your life again when he could not even fit you into his busy schedule. You were trembling with hate and helplessness. You had been made to wait to see him. You had barely entered when an anonymous voice let you know that your time was up, since his was reserved for the State from one second to the next. You were waiting for him to finish so

117

that you could say goodbye, staring at the floor, a sour taste in your mouth. Wasted: the expense of the white shirtdress with its lovely long sleeves that you were wearing, bought especially for this appointment, chosen because you knew that he would like it; a bubble-shaped dress of raw silk, the buttons in the front going down its full length so that he might open it more easily if he felt like it. Upset: all the skillful effort, patiently applied for two hours this morning to give your face the look that mingles candor and perversity which he finds so appealing. It mattered little to you that he followed the surge of tears in your frantic eyes, just to believe in his own power. He had broken you, he knew it, too; so did you. Indeed, you were completely indifferent to hearing him say to his secretary:

"All right. Please ask the Secretary General to come back this afternoon . . . He says it's urgent? . . . Not so urgent that it can't wait for a few hours . . . Yes, that's perfect, if my schedule allows it, this afternoon at three."

He came towards you, smiled at you as if to say: "You see how impressive I am." Without thinking, you gave him the recognition he was waiting for.

"Thank you . . . I am imposing on your very precious time . . ."

"No, no, come now," he protested, pleased with himself. "Let's get back to your problem. We have twenty minutes to straighten things out."

Right away you made the first move. Nervously, you asked him:

118

"Forgive me... If you still want me, I am all yours..."

He received the blow with extreme caution. In silence. All things considered, it was a kind of transformation for both of you. His game, characterized by an infantile wish to show off his power, ended by itself. He was in seventh heaven with the thought of taking you back, you cheeky little thing, of putting you in a cage. At last he would have the little canary for which he had been waiting for months. As for you, you knew that the least of your actions would have a different incentive every time. Your kindness as well as your smiles would only function as a screen.

He was pacing back and forth, relieved and feverish, a little kid happy to have been able to retrieve his toy. He voiced his feelings:

"I've been waiting for you, you know. Didn't I tell you that?"

"Yes, you did."

"I am really... well pleased that you have changed your mind."

"I have never understood what it is in me that could possibly deserve your attention."

"I love you."

"Hm!"

"Don't you believe me?"

"Yes, I do."

He stood still in front of you, raised you up from the chair, sat down where you had been sitting, taking you on his

119

knees. He was kissing you, free from restraint again, when you blurted out:

"You will find me work, won't you?"

He barely twitched, recovered quickly, and, self-possessed again, answered you as if it went without saying:

"Of course, that's imperative . . ."

Of course, that was imperative . . . You were in awe of his self-control, wondering whether he had ever thought of this seriously before your request. Having taken you for himself, he obviously had to fish you out of the gutter, clean you up, bring you out in the open, eventually heal some wounds, erase the signs of a particular past forever.

"No, why would you work? That's not at all necessary!"

He was perspiring with happiness despite the air conditioning; he was touching on plans, opening new roads, opening his heart. "I'll find you an apartment . . . No, you'll live in a furnished place I have in town . . . Don't object . . . Oh, no . . . You can't continue living in that . . . in that . . . well, where you are now . . . Your friend? I shall personally take care of it . . . I promise . . . As of tomorrow you'll have a chauffeur-driven car . . . I'll see you this evening, let's say at nine . . . You'll be settled in . . . My own driver will take you. He'll help you move . . . Stop worrying. It's easy to get lost in a large city . . . Perhaps she is in the middle of the greatest love affair of her life, while you are fretting pointlessly . . . What do you know? Yes . . . all right . . . Till tonight then . . . There's the Ambassador who's waiting . . . Quickly, get dressed . . . I'll see you later . . . Yes, yes, it's a promise . . . Nine o'clock."

It is one o'clock in the morning. Ravenously hungry, you're going in circles amid all these expensive furnishings, in a living room that is too large for you alone, a dining room that is too white, a kitchen with appliances that are too complicated. You tried to sleep, fruitlessly. Exasperated, ready to drop all these decorations and colors in order to regain the freedom of a bird in the wide-open, blue sky, you are dreaming of revenge. If only you could . . . But your own people have directed you onto a road which to you, at this hour of the night, seems an exorbitant punishment.

The apartment did not offer the restoration that you coveted when he spoke of it this morning; not even the entry into a life of luxury. Maybe you would have had more control over the flow of money represented in these furnishings and trinkets if you had spent it yourself. Perhaps then you would have liked it, remembering, for each little thing the excitement and the hesitation that would have occupied entire days; for each color, a thousand bits of advice gotten in the course of meetings, the long moments of vacillation, or of discussion with a salesman . . . No, your new domain was just a stage set which upset you a bit. It was as it should be. And since nine o'clock last night, you were waiting for the gong that would indicate the rising of the curtain.

You had imagined that you finally would be dazzled. Only here it was: stretched out on the downy bed, two bright lights on either side of your head that shone all the way down the bedhead, you were sinking down into your nightmare, your insides twisted in knots. Your father's bloody head was floating on clouds, hiding certain spots of the fabric-covered ceiling. You were struggling, vainly attempting to decipher its arabesques, were hearing sounds.

"They've killed me."

"Why, father?"

"Perhaps for you, my daughter. For all the young people, like yourself, who think only of themselves."

"Of whom should I be thinking, then?"

"Of all those who suffer every day of their lives, for no reason at all."

Your eyes wide open, you were trying with great difficulty to tear from your dozing mind, word for word, the meaning of the phrases the administrator of justice had spoken: "Shame of our tribe . . . He died for the cause of his people . . . He knew that things as they stand now are no good . . . You can be of great help to us through your politician friend . . . Our enemies are Black like us . . ." A suffocating halt to your memories: If I'd stayed in my village, would I have been more devoted? I would have married, I would have had children . . . The women of my generation are on their third one now . . . It was the predictable routine that made me flee: children, cooking, field work, the well, until the end of my days . . .

"Go, my child," the Reverend Mother Superior had urged. "You are bright. In the city, you can take up your college studies. May God bless you . . ."

Hardly three months at the university and the alarming throb of excessive freedom had conquered you. Stretched out on silk sheets, you were now awaiting your lord and master . . . The pressures on you were overwhelming. You had no clear idea for what downtrodden poor people you were living among these lovely things. In order to tear them away from their misery, you had been installed as guardian of a male's desires. Dedicated to his whims in order to avenge that mutilated head that was bouncing before you, all that was required of you was the warmth of your thighs. It was madness. But that was what your people had decided. You were the fingers of a single hand . . . The truth made you dizzy. It also justified your existence.

You will wait for him. He will surely come. You will then take his head between your hands and you will whisper with feeling:

"My love, why did you abandon me?"

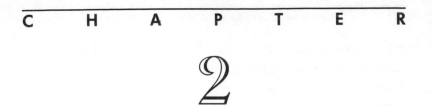

CHAPTER

2

I had neither the leisure nor the time to be moved by my victory. All afternoon I ran into windows and doors that were closed. The hours of royal tranquility were done with. I was crossing over into the battle zone.

I was in a meeting with the Secretary General of Foreign Trade, when I was called to attend a restricted meeting

124

of the Council: according to reliable information, the government would not be able to obtain the confidence of the Chambers . . . "As yet, it's only a rumor," said the President of the Council, "but from this moment on, we had better think of some concrete arrangements in order to avoid a crisis. It would be enough for us to split the opposition, for example. But how?" He was downplaying the shock, was consulting, asking for opinions and viewpoints. I was predisposed towards a surprise move. ". . . In politics there are no rumors. They always turn out to be as harmful as established facts. We have to take the lead. Break up the opposition: disconcert those members of parliament who, despite laborious subterfuges, are on the best of terms with the insurgents; in passing, compromise a few others who are playing innocent . . . ; finally, take on the young members of the group guardedly . . . Would it not actually be enough to lend them a hand, as if by chance, and make a donation, discreetly agreed upon beforehand? They would be jubilant, in the same way as any beggar to whom one might open a palace gate . . ." "To propose such methods seems so unlike you . . ." I had laid out the broad lines of a policy and generously left their imaginations free rein, just as he wanted it. And here he was congratulating me, or at least hinted at it, smiling at the cynicism with which he should have credited himself, since all I had done was interpret things his way. "But it is only reasonable, Mr. President . . ." I kept myself from adding: ". . . politics has its ways . . ."

We were studying the practical procedures by which

to split the opposition when I had to leave the session: a phone call from a distant cousin summoned me home immediately, as something terrible had happened.

The car had barely stopped in front of the porch as I opened the car door, ran up the staircase. Terror seized me as soon as I reached the French doors: the living room was swarming with people. A real marketplace: old ladies sitting right on the Oriental carpet, holding bottles of beer, were drinking and chatting away in high spirits. The dining room had been changed into a room of mourning. Piercing cries were punctuating the tribal oratory and praises of my family, contrasting with the lamentations of the hired mourners. The cries became twice as loud when I came in. Prostrate with grief, with shaven heads and bare chests, my wife and a few close relatives were the embodiment of sorrow and desolation. Overwhelmed, I pondered the stained red carpet, the deep-red ottomans that served as side tables . . .

One of my uncles took me by the shoulders and led me into my office, which had been left untouched. He made me sit down on the couch, took a chair; he announced easily:

"Your son is dead, you know that."

No, I had been sensing it since my arrival. He is dead. I tried to speak. To understand the why and the how. I spoke deep down inside myself, shocked, my thoughts shaken, screaming that it wasn't true, prepared to do anything against this misfortune. How could this happen to me, to me? He was busy explaining:

126

"It was that circumcision that was badly done. An infection not properly taken care of..."

The medical details mattered little to me.

"Come on now, you don't die from a circumcision! An infection? What infection? What infection?... So? Yes, of course. I was aware of it. Instead of going to the dispensary, my wife was using powdered charcoal to heal the wound better... It is the most effective medication... You don't die of that..." What I found absolutely senseless was the very notion of circumcision. It was she who had first brought it up. Sooner or later she will pay. Yes, my dear companion, I hate you!

I was outlining projects, but with each new step I was running into him: my little cowboy. His eyes were shining as always when he was at the peak of excitement.

"Come, daddy, be the horse!" I would pretend to scowl. He would climb up on me, start yelling: "Ho, ho, I am the Lone Ranger... Giddyap... You are my Jolly Jumper... Away we go... The bandits of Abilene are mine."

After five minutes, I would beg quite frankly: "The horse is tired. Very tired..."

He would object, my little cowboy, he would fume. I would explain: "... Listen, I have a lot to do... In return, I promise that I'll tell you a wonderful story before bedtime..." He would roll on the floor, scream... I would threaten him, jokingly: "Bandits of Abilene, come and look at

127

the cowboy, come and see your fearful enemy. . ." It worked every time. He would stop his lunges, would roll around a few minutes, then would join me in my office, all his dignity restored.

"Be nice, daddy, tell me a story. A nice story about cowboys. With a lot of mean Indians and bad bandits."

I would make it up. Distractedly. He hung on every word, would stop me regularly: "What does that mean, what you just said?" It was an obsession with him. Happy, he would nod his head in approval, pleased with the cowboys; disappointed, he would point his index finger to my nose: ". . . You know, daddy, that's not possible because the other day you said . . ."

Little argumentative god. Exactly. It wasn't possible. You were nothing but a small body, dry and cold in an enormous bed. A small black angel face, solidified by magic spells, a small forehead that was too peaceful, hued in browns by strips of greyish light, the dusk that was coming through the pale curtains. You are sweet, my cowboy.

"My little cowboy doesn't need two pillows. I'll take one. It's mine. Look, it's a ball, a ball of fire. It's going to roll through the streets and all the cars will let it through . . ." We would burst out laughing. "Now you're going to sleep, my bandit. I'm turning off the light." "Don't close the door, daddy!" "All right, my cowboy . . . Good night." In this bed of inlaid wood, the tints of which had been worn down, you looked relaxed. Tears of helplessness were welling up. Outside, the rain was falling. I don't know how, I had the defi-

nite impression that it was part of the secret. But which one?
A warning sign, without question. For what reason can one
die at the age of four? Why, God of my Ancestors, why?

Yet, one year ago, his grandmother had consecrated
him during the holidays. He had come back thrilled, a little
thinner but full of vitality. His mother was delighted.

"Daddy, when can I go back to grandmama? You
know, she gave me a white chicken, just for me alone. Her
wings were tied. I played with her all day long . . ."

Already I thought of the following day: I would free
myself after the burial to take the reins again. Time off to
mourn? Absolutely not, not now. That would be admitting
that I was vulnerable. I needed to react, to direct, to be on
top of the political chicaneries. I would have liked to direct
the action against the opposition.

"Daddy, grandmama killed the chicken. My own
chicken. I didn't want to eat her. She was my friend. My
mama told me that I had to, to be strong like you. So I ate it.
Because you know, daddy, when I'm big I'm going to be like
you. I'm going to be a government minister, too. And have
an even bigger car than yours . . ."

"You did well, my cowboy. You'll be big, very big
and strong; stronger that me . . ."

At this point, I tried to identify with the tidal wave
that was rising from the depths of my being. I had to succeed
in taking my revenge, and, to do so, I had to submit first of
all to the ritual, to bend my rigidities to the promptings of
my instinct. For two days, hour after hour, I searched among

the set faces of those offering me their condolences for the one responsible for my misfortune. After the burial, the young priest who had celebrated the funeral mass and given absolution wanted to distract me from my sorrows: "The ways of the Lord are unfathomable." He was honest. I wondered if these ways were the same as those of the Ancestors. Was it in vain that the latter had promised to take me under their protection?

"Take care of yourself," my uncle advised me. "Wait until the period of mourning is over before taking on your work again."

"That's not possible. Are you aware of what's happening in the government?"

"No. I hear rumors. Like everybody else. Is anything in particular going on?"

"Three days from now, the government might not have the vote of confidence of parliament . . . Take care of my wife and children. They need you. And let me do what I must do . . ."

He most certainly understood that if I ceased to be Minister of State, he would feel a little diminished. My private secretary, who, settled in my office, was answering condolence calls and letters throughout the day, seemed to my uncle to be one of the measures of my power, in which he, too, was a participant. That I was hungering to live according to my dreams, convinced that I had a national destiny, an ancestral mission, was my private concern which I could not reveal to him: he would think me mad, he who has always allowed himself to be carried along by the flow of things.

I thought of my beloved, gave thanks to that mysterious rift that had brought her back to me. I had forgotten her. A telephone call. She understood, sympathized with me, told me she had waited throughout the night, begged me to come by for just five minutes; I promised.

Despite my incessant comings and goings between the Ministry and the house, the house and the office of the President of the Council, intellectually I was sinking into an odd depression, accentuated by the rituals of mourning every evening: inside the house, the women with naked torsos, engulfed in their cries and sobs; in the yard, the men drinking and laughing. It was a corrosive that made a direct attack on my little cowboy. Lightning had struck me. I needed to straighten up again, sink roots, grow still stronger. I said so to the Master.

"I no longer expect the kindness of those close to me."

"Does that surprise you?"

"Yes, it amazes me."

Mysterious, his inscrutable look seemed moved by a presence behind me. In a choking voice he spoke again:

"How much of a signal do you need to understand that one cannot make light of the Ancestors?"

I thought of the sacrifice, of the promise I had made and not yet kept because I had not had the time. Deeply stirred, I questioned:

"It isn't you, is it, who has struck me down?"

From his full height he gazed at me, undecided, cold. He put his hand on my shoulder. I began to fear his strength.

"No, my son. It is not we who did it. For us, it is a terrible sign to which we must respond and by unmasking as quickly as possible the one who did strike your son. We will then be able to react, with the help of God . . . But you ought to learn not to joke about either the sacrifices or the servants of God . . ."

My inordinate absentmindedness seemed monstrous to me in the face of the Master's demand. It was pointless to indulge in explanations. On the spot I signed a check, made out to him, for one and a half million francs. It was as it should be. I needed to avenge the sudden departure of my son and to remain under the protective privileges of the gods.

"Peace be with you, my son; and may the Ancestors be within you."

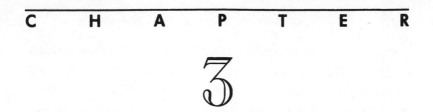

C H A P T E R

3

"Do you understand? With this death I completely lost my head."

"Yes, I know, but . . . I missed you so badly."

"Please forgive me, Beauty."

You forgave him, delighted to still have that as a re-

133

source to forget your anger. After all, the death of a son was a serious matter . . . "This evening," he had told you, "we'll forget all misfortune to celebrate our reconciliation." "Yes, that would be lovely." And happy, joy having returned, you had once again found your appetite for whimsy on the dance floor. Your body, free after this long period of indolence, eagerly loosened with the music. Cautious, a flash of mischief in his eyes, he followed your steps, a good student, gifted and lithe, despite his incipient stoutness. He was handsome, you thought, a purebred animal, with the strong neck of a rhinoceros. "What do you think I look like?" he had asked you once. "You have the vigor and the strength of a buffalo or a rhinoceros," you had replied. He had smiled, both flattered and disappointed. Now you knew why: he loves to play the refined diplomat . . .

Was it his neck's brandish or the daring of your inner maledictions which gave you your new self-assurance? When you arrived at the bar, looking magnificent, you had ignored your old friends, the dance hostesses. "If they have no kingdom, let them go on begging, just as I did."

He had agreed with you. Back within your own thoughts, you knew that for the first time in your life you were truly envied and undoubtedly hated as well.

"I must set myself apart from them," you had told him, choosing a light-colored stole which, though it still left your shoulders bare, gave you the look of an aristocrat.

"You are a living sculpture," he had answered, his eyes blurred, gazing upon you as if you were a statue.

Dinner had been sumptuous, as it always was with him. He made a flamboyant banquet out of the least meal. He said that he came from a godly breed and ostentation was his universe. He neither wanted nor was able to lower himself. As usual, you two were the center of attention in the restaurant. The waiters were fluttering around your table, humble and efficient servants. Despite your reservations, you admired his disposition: to take you out in public, before the eyes of the whole city, less than one week after the death of his son, while his wife was still in mourning . . .

You had barely started eating when you had to respond to a veritable interrogation that dealt as much with your secret wishes as with your tastes, your friendships and other regular company you kept, your family and your political opinions. You were playing the silly little ingenue, and each time you brought the conversation back to your love for him and his generosity towards you. You were grateful to him. In return, he overwhelmed you with compliments, itemizing each physical detail, dwelling emphatically on your amber necklace, the golden bracelets that made the smallest motion of your arms sing. He had the eye of an owner looking over a new animal acquired at a steep price. When the moment seemed right to you, you asked whether there was any news about your friend and her disappearance.

"I don't understand it at all," he explained, a sincere look in his eyes. "I promised you that I would follow the whole thing through and very closely at that. And I have . . . The police commissioner who's in charge wonders if your

135

friend might not have simply gone back to her village . . .
How can we know, though, since your region is fully occupied by the rebels . . ."

He lightly shrugged his shoulders and then, teas-
ingly, made the attack: "I certainly hope that you're not planning on joining her there, with the rebels?"

"Do I look like a rebel?"

And your throaty laughter rose, ringing with candor.
His theory was plausible, you felt yourself reviving, one
thing less to worry about. He continued talking, thrilled to
have amused you with a funny comment, he was telling you
about the rebellion. You kept him going:

"It seems that you are having problems in the government . . ."

You offered him another, more certain opening. He
took it without hesitation, began to hold forth on the tactless-
ness of certain politicians, the unseemliness of the principle of
democracy Western-style.

". . . Power is a consecration. It should be reserved
for a few who are chosen by the gods . . . The people have
never ruled, not anywhere . . ." He was juggling words you
had trouble understanding, ideas that were disorienting.
". . . Isn't it unthinkable that, through a mere accident or
some glorification, just any person can get himself elected or
give birth to a child? They're democratically mimicking the
princely virtues . . . It's scandalous!" Floodgates had opened.
You suspected a trap somewhere, but had no inkling of where

to detect it . . . Besides, it didn't matter much to you. You should let him talk, and in passing you would learn what was of interest to you. Furthermore, when he was speaking he was appreciative of the silence of others, especially of women. ". . . You are an exceptional woman . . . You, at least, know how to listen . . ." You made a sound, laughing brightly, a good little plaything, and brought him back on track again:

"But what do you expect to do, then, to squash the rebellion? Isn't it becoming worrisome?"

He started back on the avenues his mind had taken, unveiling dark alleyways, hidden inclines, quoting names to impress you, uncovering secret and tortuous paths, finally announcing the salvation of the Republic. You were listening, won over by so much innocence, but frightened as well, by the violence brought to light. To reward him you had suggested that you dance.

"Would that please you, my prince?"

Playfully he had kissed you, lifting you despite the circling of other dancers, slightly drunk with his own words, the champagne, the very atmosphere of the bar. A few days away from this place was an eternity; this was where you had learned what it means to be alive. Here you had found again the shimmering of solitary and enchanted islands. Your moist body brushing against his, first surprised, then overwhelmed, you were witnessing the birth of a desire that astonished you. Excited, you began to murmur the lyrics which held you riveted to each other in a rumba by Franco:

137

O ma makambo éé
O ma makambo éé

Likambo ya ngana soki omoni
Bombaka na motema
Ekolaka ndongo bandeko éé

O ma makambo éé
O ma makambo éé

The minuscule dance floor had become a footbridge. Everywhere else the passage was blocked: smiles on your lips, you were bending and swaying, forwards and backwards, trying, with a step to the left, a bending to the right, to stay in time with the beat of the drum and the deep bass of a masterly guitar. Dancing in the rhythm of blood, bewildered, you were wondering if this was not the very instant in which you would sell out your own people to their enemies . . .

Your composure restored, you were discovering him to be less loathsome than you had claimed; you feigned coldness which, for the sake of your own conscience, was to cover up the rush you felt.

At your small table in the semidarkness, you were watching him avidly; eager to know him to be yours and worried to think that you might lose him some day. You held out your hand to him, hoping in this way, in the exaltation of a night out, to break the evil spell of your people just for a

138

moment. You were caught in the storm, feverish, living pure joy. You shuddered when he approached.

"Happy to see you, my girl. How are you? They told me I'd find you here . . . Good evening, Sir."

"This is the Minister of . . ."

You were stammering, apologized, a bad little girl, caught in the act. Then: "My dear, this is an uncle of mine. He's in business."

"Don't I get a kiss?" your uncle resumed.

Cursing silently, you brought yourself to do as you were asked, smiling, turning first one cheek and then the other to him, asking him in a whisper to come by your place as quickly as possible, preferably in the morning after ten. Your man had become aloof, watching the musicians who were vigorously playing a dance called the jerk. He had perfected the art of putting both you and your uncle ill at ease. You cleared your throat.

"Darling . . ."

He turned his head, superb in his arrogance. Your uncle was taking his leave. Man of the world, he urged through clenched teeth:

"Please sit down with us. Of course, I'm delighted to meet you . . . Your niece must be so pleased . . ."

Your uncle excused himself with the same hypocrisy.

"That's very kind of you . . . No, really . . . I am here with friends . . . Have fun, little one . . . Why don't you come home and visit us from time to time?" He left, rejoined a group of men and women sitting in the back of the bar.

"Let's leave," he said.

"Already? I was just beginning to have a good time."

"Doesn't your uncle's presence bother you?"

"Sure it does. But that's no reason to go running off as if the place is on fire."

Soothed, he offered you another glass of champagne. You took his hands in yours again. He did not resist, with closed eyes he was dreaming of God knows what beautiful or horrendous things. You knew now that he was a jealous beast; that you should never again provoke him with foolish uncles.

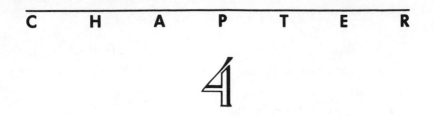

e had rung the doorbell with an urgency that was completely out of order. Furious, she opened the door a crack, then recognizing him immediately, she forgot her anger and invited him in. He entered. Her eyes followed the footprints of his heavy, dusty shoes. Level-headed, a subservient smile on her lips, she asked him to sit down. He dropped into an easy chair with the grace of an elephant. And commanded:

"Get me a drink, will you, Ya?"

He looked like someone who hadn't slept in many days: his skin leathery, eyelids swollen, his face drawn.

"Ya," he said roughly, "are you sure he's not going to come back any minute?"

She thought it strange that a man his age and with his experience could so naively express his fear and worry about trivia. Politely she replied:

"I don't think he'll be back. He told me that he had a great deal of work at the Ministry. And then I believe I heard him say there was a Council meeting around ten o'clock. Don't be afraid. The only thing I expect is a phone call just before nine-thirty."

"Who said I was afraid?"

With his drink in her hand, she stood still for a moment, then put it on a side table close to his chair.

"Perhaps you aren't afraid, but I am. I live in a state of constant fear. You understand? I asked you to come by after ten . . . It is barely nine o'clock . . . What if you had run into each other? I would also appreciate it if you wouldn't approach me again when I am with him. He is a very jealous man . . ."

"The perfect husband . . . And the browbeaten wife!"

What a brute, she thought. She understood that it was very much in her interest to keep her nerves under control.

142

Keeping her manner pleasant, she ignored the irony and replied calmly:

"He is not my husband. Not yet, in any event. He does want to marry me; did you know that?"

He didn't flinch; he ran his eyes over the furniture and the paintings with an indifferent look, tired, incapable of showing any emotion.

"You sure provide a topic for conversation. You are seen together all over town. We were not aware that your seductiveness was such as to make him lose all sense of discretion!"

"But I'm just following orders . . ."

"True enough. But you weren't asked to drive him crazy the way you're doing. You're seen together everywhere . . . Soon some smart aleck is going to ask himself a few questions: they don't come from the same tribe, the girl's father was a notorious rebel leader . . . Can't you see that coming?"

"Yes . . ."

She felt oppressed by a strange sense of turmoil. She remained nonplussed. Her eyes went over his worn collar, the jacket he had taken off, and his dusty pants without really noticing them. She knew that he was right, wondered whether one day she would be able to cross the demarcation line that separated her from these men who, at every step, were able to foresee the consequences of each of their actions. With tears in her eyes she left the living room, returning after a few minutes, having changed her robe to a neat, light-colored suit of silk serge.

She plugged in the record player, put on the first record she found, turned the volume up as high as it would go, and sat down next to him. The voice of Philippe Lavil shook the house.

I don't know, with girls, I don't know
When you should or should not
When you should not
Talk of the weather or of love . . .

"Good point," he said without a smile. "But do you actually think the house is bugged? Who would have put them there?"

"My friend the Minister, for instance . . ."

She could now see him sideways: his eyes had become smaller, his eyelids were fluttering as if a light wind were moving them. She wanted to score another point.

"Please note that it's a little late . . . If there is a bug, it has surely registered the lecture you just gave me . . . It would be enough to send me to my death."

He completely ignored her reaction. "How about telling me what you know."

In his eyes, she thought, I am worthless. I could disappear and nothing would change. She wanted to despise him, studied him carefully: the face which in the half-light of the bar had seemed firm and strong to her now appeared flabby, pathetic enough to be pitiful. Were it not for his calm and nasty look, she would have taken him for an old bum pretending to be frightening. She began to speak, determined to shock him:

". . . The government is actually going to undertake a twofold action fairly soon. In the capital, they're going to put pressure on the opposition. Two objectives: first of all, to break it up, to cause the group to splinter into many little factions; secondly, to put those parliament members who are suspected of supporting you on the spot once and for all . . . As for the rebellious provinces, a decisive attack is in preparation. It will be a massive one; it is to begin in the next few days, as soon as the government will have obtained the parliament's vote of confidence . . ."

She was now a smoothly running machine, a little computer without feeling that was putting forth a political future. The plans in progress came tumbling out, one after the other, precise, numbered, in the finest detail, just as she had learned or deduced them. She was divulging the sources, the names of those people to be eliminated from action as quickly as possible, the ties to be severed; then, facing an imaginary military map, she pointed out what the present forces were, and step by step, she outlined the route of the reconquering troops, the number of batallions, the projected strategies . . .

As she was speaking, she looked him straight in the eye. Looking indifferent, seemingly callous, he was observing her as she sipped her drink. Certain that she deserved good marks, she ended with some personal thoughts:

"To tell you the truth, I have the feeling we're heading for a bloodbath . . ."

He didn't budge. In a toneless voice he said:

"You're only asked to communicate facts, not your state of mind. Do you know how many on our side have already died?"

"No."

"Neither do I. Because they can't be counted any more. So don't interfere by giving us lessons in political action."

She didn't see the blow coming. Flat out on the carpet, she gasped with rage. She was perfectly willing to recognize her wrongs, but she couldn't see why all these men gave themselves the right to brutalize her every time they felt like it, just because they were involved in a struggle to the death. The last time, she had been left covered with bruises for weeks. She had believed that the dishonor she had brought upon her people might justify them. But this little twerp gave himself permission to lay a hand on her by invoking some fictional impertinence. Effortlessly, she got up again, leaned her elbows on an easy chair, looked at him with contempt.

"My fine sir! I hope that calmed you down. I ask you just one thing: to get out of that door and not to put your feet inside it anymore . . . Ever again. You understand?"

He got up, began to walk towards her. She backed away as far as the chest of drawers, grabbed the receiver of

146

the phone, dialed a number . . . He stopped in the middle of the room.

"Put that down, little girl, this is ridiculous. You don't know me . . . Do you even know my name? No. So who are you going to call? The police? They won't come . . . They never come, for that matter . . . Your politician? Before he gets here with his private cops, I'd be able to kill you and get out of here without any difficulty whatsoever . . ."

He was watching her, calmly, as if she were nothing but a bothersome little insect. She put the receiver back with trembling hands, sat down in the nearest chair. He came and stood in front of her.

"Listen to me, little girl. I won't come back to your house. That's one thing. Not because you demand it, but because I'm careful."

He fished a cigarette butt out of his pocket and stuck it between his lips. She considered pointing to the bucket filled with packs of cigarettes, but decided not to. She could feel the tension rising, knew, as he did, that the moment of truth had arrived. Frozen in place, she watched him light his cigarette butt, then go to the window. He placed himself against the light.

"Understand that you're not worth a whole lot. I would almost like to help you die. You and your people, all of you with your fine words, you make me sick . . . This tribal rebellion, shoveling out its incomprehensible verbiage, you want me to tell you what I think of it? You want me to?"

She wished she would faint or simply collapse just to escape from him one way or another. Her head began to spin, the room began to sway, she thought she saw him upside down, feet in the air, then the very next moment he was right in front of her, hands in his pockets.

"A rebellion for smalltime assholes... Yes... tribes grown fanatic, darts in their hands, who throw themselves at cannons aided and abetted by proletarian slogans... For what?"

Each word cut through her, a flaming blade through her entrails. She knew that everything was lost, but hung on. An irrepressible force kept her from screaming. She wanted to know. Everything.

"What did your father know about the proletariat? Can you tell me that? What did he want? Wait, I'll tell you ... His piece of the pie is what he wanted... Just like all those brainless morons who, by dint of their fantasies, manipulate the rank stupidity of the peasants... Who's getting killed? Go see who's dying! You, you expected better, didn't you? To direct the revolution. And now the whores are getting mixed up in it, too... Long live the revolution!"

She had slid off the chair. She was struggling to keep her thoughts together, to climb back up the slope, in vain ... A ghastly pain had moved into her chest. In a dream, she saw her father's head meandering around again, the laughingstock of the village kids. Then came the stakes that perforated his kidneys. A long time later, she thought she heard herself moan.

148

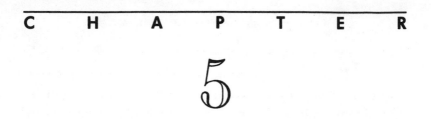

C H A P T E R

5

"Tell me..."

He had that slightly
tipsy look which I knew him to have almost every evening.
In my nightgown, sitting cross-legged on my bed, the sleep
still in my eyes, I was watching him. He had dropped into
the chair crying out:

"What luck that you're here!"

Then he had gotten up again, had taken off his jacket which he flung down at random. I was feeling very much at ease in my role as faithful little dog awaiting her master's return. "Well, here I am . . . You, at least, understand my distress when I need it." He brought me a glass of orange juice.

"Drink," he told me, "it will do you a lot of harm . . ."

He burst out laughing. I began to drink, pleased to see him in a happy mood. He appeared to be in a state of grace, brought me confidence and joy. He made a suggestion:

"Before I forget, I have been invited to a cocktail party tomorrow . . . I'm going to take you out into official public life for the first time . . . And this time you're coming . . ."

"Please talk to me . . . Was dinner good? Were there many women, were they beautiful? Whom did you see? What did you do?"

He began to talk and, at last, I felt life returning to me. The sun came out of his mouth, was warming me. I let myself go, carried away by his words. I was taken beyond all boundaries, liberated. He had the strength and the tenacity that it took to rivet me to his side. And that was all I was looking for. Overpowered, I let myself go, satisfied. He was talking to me . . .

That morning, he had phoned me later than usual. Self-contained, unself-conscious, light-headed, he had announced to me that the government had received the vote of confidence from parliament without any problem. He gave himself the credit for it, held forth on the people's new destiny. The word "people" made me jump. I had thought of complaining to him, of telling him my tale of woe, disclosing to him what had happened to me. He didn't give me a chance. He was talking to me of destinies and thereby affirmed my role as the good little wife, without any problems of her own, held aloft by the success of her man.

"I am taking you out tonight... We're going to the dinner given by the President of the Council in honor of our victory... It's a dinner for more than five hundred guests ... Of all the women there, you'll be the most beautiful, won't you?"

He had not bothered to ask me whether I felt like going out. He had simply straddled his dream. I needed only to bend to his wishes, to be grateful to him for the fancies that, as always, centered around him. The visit of "my uncle" had wiped me out.

"No, please, not tonight. I really don't feel up to it. You go by yourself and have a good time; really, enjoy yourself... Promise? Then when you get back, wake me up and tell me all about it... Swear that you will?"

Full of charm, he had insisted, trying to prove to me how important this introduction would be, enumerating the celebrities that would be there. Then, suddenly, he had begun to concern himself with my discomfort, recommended some medication and rest. Coyly, I minimized my pain.

151

"It's nothing, really. I'm going to rest, do nothing all day. Maybe I'll take a walk later this afternoon. I'll go to bed early tonight. But do wake me when you come home . . ."

He was now taking care of me, explaining that he had been hesitant to wake me. But since he had sworn that he would . . . A true father. Looking as if he were apologetic for having gone to the party, he questioned me:

"And you, Beauty?"

"Me?"

"What did you do? You weren't too bored?"

The morning came back to me. I wanted to tell him that I'd been . . . I had been what? It was ludicrous. I would have to provide him with reasons, fabricate new lies. To what end? I was half asleep, feeling good in the fog that enveloped me. He came to sit down on the bed. His hand was lightly stroking my chest. I stretched out and found the tepid groove that my body had left. With sensuous ease, I answered:

"Can't you tell? . . . I've done nothing but take care of my body . . . In bed all morning. This afternoon I took a long walk . . ."

The streets were deserted. Ngombe, calm little community within Kinshasa's noise, an old residential section that used to be reserved for Europeans only, was now a sort of park, with tree-lined streets and avenues, gardens one chances upon at traffic circles. In these lovely lanes, I had felt like a little girl playing hooky from school. Attentive only to my mood and the weight of my soul, I had sat on a bench for several hours facing the immense, flowing river, all muscle and sinew, the color of flesh.

He came and lay down next to me, fully dressed. He put an arm under my neck. He was breathing heavily. With one finger, he was caressing my shoulder. With bent head, I was watching his gently lighted face. The light brought out his features, marked by fatigue.

"You look like a musketeer."

"What?"

"I said that you are my musketeer."

"And you, you are my beloved Beauty, the only one . . ."

"Yes?"

I was imagining him in a fray, his torso naked, a fierce look on his face, a sword in his hand, cutting off heads to present them all bloody to me. I was beginning to feel nauseated as I carefully traced each feature of his face, his high forehead that hid an entire world.

"Are you dreaming of murder, my musketeer?"

"Yes."

"Do you want to kill? To massacre them all?"

I realized that I was tiring him out. I knew what his response was. We were both driven by the same diabolical force. He had a rank to defend and knew quite well how to do it. I would scream my rage at him, and it would come back to me, toned down by his derision, I was sure. You are a luxurious interlude, I thought. My eyes were closed, I believe, but my lips slightly open. I felt his middle finger gently caressing them.

Through some strange bit of irony, my thoughts led me to probe a dreadful memory just then. I was finishing my last year of secondary school when he had come into my life.

"I love you. Could you become the mother of my children?"

"Right away?"

"Yes. As soon as you finish high school."

Nice little guy. According to tradition, he had remitted the first part of the dowry. My parents had accepted it. I was therefore reserved for him. In the meantime he continued to beg me, in all sincerity, looking as if he believed that I was able to turn his plans upside down. Had he not done that, then perhaps I would now be his wife, as my people had wanted it. "Are you going to marry him?" "No, Reverend Mother. I would like to go on with my studies..." "You are right, my daughter. When you marry a young man your own age one day, you'll be happy that you were able to study. And, then, to be the wife of a polygamist..."

He used to bring me fresh corn as school let out, I would thank him, take his presents home. It was not a good match because he was over forty years old, while I was barely nineteen. It was not a good match because he was a polygamist... A question of common sense, what else!

"How old are you, my musketeer?"

"Thirty-five. Why?"

"I'm twenty-five and I think you're marvelous."

Although I had been forced into his life, I recognize that I am pleased to be there. Our ages, our spirits, and our bodies are in tune. I took his hand and pressed it tightly.

"Tell me . . ."

"What?"

"What happened to your wife?"

"She left for the village."

"Why?"

"First of all, because she is a sorceress. It is she who's responsible for the death of my son . . ."

"And why else?"

"And then, because I love you."

"For how long?"

"I don't know . . . In any case, whatever happens, I shall always consider you a privileged friend . . ."

He is speaking in a soft, tired voice. Soon he is going to sink into sleep. Just as I'm coming out of it. Hold on to him? Little by little, I felt a weight of hatred for my people forming inside of me, and I felt it with pleasure. If I asked, would my musketeer protect me against them?

"Are you really sure your wife is a sorceress?"

"Yes."

"How can you be?"

He answered with a grunt. He had fallen asleep. After turning off the lights, I tried to reason with myself. My father had taught me that only I could live with my spirits. Why then force this outsider to preoccupy himself with my dead? His wife was a sorceress, he had confirmed that. It was more than a signal he had given me. I would have to recoup the support from my own people if I wanted to survive him. Grateful, I caressed his face. Tomorrow, I said to myself as I curled up, tomorrow I shall be beautiful. He will be proud of me.

IV

1

Dusk was crumbling away when the two of you arrived. The large Mercedes rolled right up to the stoop. The chauffeur got out to open the car door for him; "Don't let go of me," you wanted to say, but he had already turned his face. A white servant opened the car door for you, bowed down deeply.

"Madame."

He walked around the car to join you, his well-developed torso showing, a smile on his lips.

"Is Beauty worried?"

"Yes, my musketeer. Don't leave me alone, not even for a second, please. I'd be too scared."

Smiling, you held out your hand to him, thinking that, with time, the permanent lacerations inside you would become pleasant afflictions, if only you could merit his devotion for a long time to come.

The Ambassador welcomed you, all sugar and honey. Like a butler. The Ambassador's wife swept you away —"Please come this way, my dear lady... We'll be more comfortable. The gentlemen will be joining us..." You exchanged some small talk.

Plenty of indications, you thought worriedly, revealed your discomfort. Reticent, humble, naive, a little awkward, nervous fingers on the golden clasps that held your dress in place, you answered questions with a faint detachment, the look of a schoolgirl facing favorable examiners. Your youth was your weapon; your beauty a symbol for having led you across a long obstacle course all the way into the receiving room of one of the world's most powerful nations, where you were being welcomed with open arms. In the torpor that numbed you as you recalled your father's memory, you were trying to understand the way in which these elderly white ladies were enemies of your people.

With a smile on your lips, you thought you were

being drowned. Then you saw him coming, hands on his back, the contained look of an animal tamer. He reclaimed you with poise: with some beautiful commonplaces, gently spoken, for the ladies, he put an end to the anguish of a victory that ill suited you.

"I'm not happy, my musketeer. You promised not to leave me for a second," you whispered in his ear.

Couples were introduced to you. Well-known names: His Excellency the Ambassador of . . . and Mrs . . . , His Excellency the Consul of . . . and Mrs . . . , the President of . . . and Mrs . . . He responded with a word or a sentence, made some inquiries, asked after the person's health, while you, with a tight smile, were hesitant, did not know what to say. You were discovering a resplendent world, altogether different from your own; a world of which you had had no idea until now, except through the newspapers and the radio. You nearly knelt down before the Papal Nuncio. The manner in which he approached him shocked you: he treated the Vatican's representative as if he were a traveling companion, asked him about his ulcer.

He behaved as if he were the host of the cocktail party, kept coming and going. You had hardly caught your breath before he led you away towards other guests. Glasses of whiskey appeared in your hand as if by magic and disappeared as soon as they were empty. You were speechless, and your embarrassment had the grace of a modest vanity.

A circle had formed around the two of you. You were standing in front of a mass of pink laurels. Soft music floated in the air. You watched him play his game, discover questions through smiles and silences. You knew that the protection of a Prince had been entrusted to you. You saw him disappear, in conversation with someone you did not know. A few minutes later, he gently pulled you by the arm. You turned around just a little.

"Madame?"

You laughed: you had recognized your master's voice. He was bored, he said. You were surprised that he had found a way to both uphold appearances and yet re-create his real self within this enchanting atmosphere. A French couple were trying to have a discussion with him. You distinctly heard him introduce you, between two sentences directed at the husband.

"My wife . . ."

Then came the compliments. You merely fluttered your eyelashes to thank them, your heart quickening. Words rushed out, plans for a trip. You listened to him direct the conversation, ask questions.

"So, you are leaving on vacation next week?—For the Middle East? That's wonderful!—Oh, I see, for Lebanon? Do you expect to be at the Festival of Baalbek in August? That is marvelous, you know . . . Yes, I've been there. And then there are the excavations at Tyre and the Castle of the Sea to visit . . . Not at Byblos, but at the harbor of Sidon . . ."

You tried to reconstruct a geographical map from memory in order to follow the conversation. They were going too fast; you gave up.

With the help of the alcohol, voices had lifted a few tones. You recognized a former classmate. She was now the wife of a government official. You considered joining her. But how to reach her? It would require plowing through the crowd to join her near the table with the bottles and siphons. Instinctively, you knew that it was her responsibility to come to you, given the rank of your man. Without a doubt, she was jealous. You smiled. He was talking politics.

". . . Nonalignment," he explained to a fat, bald European, who nodded his head in agreement with every word, "is a principle. It is a manner of nonconformism in relation to Western orthodoxies. We have nothing against the East; we also know that the West needs us as much as we need it, if not more so. So we proportion our friendships . . ."

Waiters were coming and going, trays in hand. You nibbled from each platter, changed from whiskey to a glass of champagne. The liquor began to give you a kind of courage, when you saw His Eminence the Archbishop approaching you. He greeted you with a chilly hand. You bowed your head slightly, gave him a bewitching smile, marveling at your own lack of fear. Yet, the Reverend Mothers had certainly introduced you to the intricacies of the Catholic hierarchy: as a schoolgirl, you used to place the Archbishop only a few degrees below God Himself. You saw him there, two steps away from you, a small, slender man with a haggard face. You would have liked to know whether he, too, had been drinking, whether he was feeling euphoric, and what he thought of this monster-sized cocktail party. He spoke in a deep, unctuous voice that clashed with the slightness of his body, which one might take to be floating inside the cassock.

"Is this your new wife?"

"Yes, Monseigneur."

"Well, well," the Bishop said in a distant voice, "you really do like change . . ."

"My first wife was a sorceress. If you see what I mean?"

He spoke, looking the Prelate straight in the eye, his cheeks tight with the obligatory smile. He took the responsibility for dialogue upon himself.

"How are your missionary posts in the occupied regions, Monseigneur?"

"We have little news," the prelate answered. "But what measures does the government plan to take?"

"Direct intervention, Monseigneur. That is the only solution. Blood will flow. There will be casualties. That is too bad, but what can one expect? We must safeguard the integrity of the national territory at any cost; defend it against those . . . They're communists, you do know that?"

"So they say, but what does that mean according to you?"

You pretended respectful boredom, following with one seemingly inattentive ear a conversation that you wished were unimportant. You focused in on certain words, a few phrases, some facts, plans to be worked out, wondering whether he was telling the truth or giving the Archbishop a coded message. In an unexpected manner he attacked:

"Monseigneur, it seems that many members of the Church have compromised themselves with those communists . . ."

The Archbishop had a peculiar talent for detecting a trap. Calmly he answered:

"Your Excellency, you say it seems . . . I only fear that they are living in a particularly delicate situation . . ."

Feeling sure, you intervened.

"My dear, the Monseigneur is right. Just the other day, my uncle was saying . . ."

He smiled at you. The Bishop looked at you without interest but also without surprise, seeking to read your eyes. Self-conscious, you smiled and made the ice cubes in your glass tinkle, to cover up your lack of composure. As a waiter passed by, you handed him your glass. The Monseigneur was taking his leave, calling you "my daughter," insisting on knowing your name.

Your man reclaimed you. "Shall we go? It's almost eight o'clock." Excited, you acquiesced. "Yes, let's leave. It was wonderful . . ." Hands to be shaken, smiling to be done. You were constructing a novel around this first introduction into the official world with him, amazed by all the attention you had received and troubled by a secret you had to keep; a secret that, in the long run, would have to destroy not only the man by your side, but perhaps also a certain number of these good people whom you had found to be so kind.

In the car that drove you home, he took you by the shoulders.

"Darling, I am proud of you."

"Me too, I am happy with you, my musketeer. You are so . . . so seductive. You know. . ."

"What?"

"I love you, my musketeer."

Deeply moved, he looked at you.

"Really?"

"Yes. I would like to be yours forever. Forever. Do you understand?"

He had moved his hand along your arm. Just a light stroking. With one finger, he began to climb up, all the way up to the bend in your arm, then down again. You wanted to measure the meaning of his look. You felt free, marvelously free. But he?

"Yes, I understand," he said.

You were struggling, your eyes burning, your body suddenly contracted. Yet, I betray him constantly . . . The soft purring of the car. The cool wind coming in. The alcohol. You felt ethereal.

"No, my musketeer, you don't understand."

Anguish, impatience. You needed to know what to do, which persona to assume. Fully attentive, he was caressing your arm. A veritable state of siege.

"Why wouldn't I understand?"

Sell him out or protect him? His hand weighed on you, gently. Night had fallen now. The fact that this party had thrilled you gave you the impression of having crossed a

BEFORE THE BIRTH OF THE MOON

threshold. Since when? Your lips trembled. Suddenly you needed him and you pressed his hand.

"Probably because you don't know me, musketeer."

"Oh, come now . . . Look here, life is very simple. I love you, you love me, we love each other. That's all that matters, isn't it?"

He laughed, withdrew into his own thoughts, happy to have removed a false barrier once and for all. But how could you believe him? Was it that difficult for him to understand that reducing a relationship to this kind of verbal conjugation was impossible?

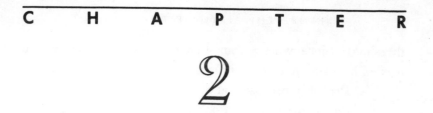

2

There were only three of them around a small round table covered with green upholstery fabric. It was a restricted meeting of the Council. The President, in a bad mood, was reviewing the different problems posed by the rebellion. He dwelled on the incomprehensible advances made by the insurgent troops; he got

168

up, pointer in hand, to comment on their movements on a survey map that hung behind him, sat down again after his exposition, grumbling between his teeth. Then, abruptly, he flew into a rage: hands shaking, he took a newspaper out of his briefcase and threw it on the table.

"Now the colonialists are getting mixed up in it. They no longer teach us any lessons . . . No, we used not to accept those too graciously. They're singing the praises of what those gangs of murderers have accomplished . . . Just look at this . . ."

He was feeling calm, surprised that, at this point, the President of the Council could not control himself any better. He remembered a lesson taught him by the Master: "Calm is a true mark of royalty under all circumstances." Since nobody spoke, he took the newspaper and read the article in question out loud.

> Paris, July 29—The National Congolese Army has ceased to exist. This is the conclusion to be drawn from the latest military operations in the Congo, after a third front was opened at Bolobo.
>
> On Tuesday, the Congolese exiles of Brazzaville succeeded in their "Bay of Pigs." Coming from what was formerly the French Congo, they crossed the river and disembarked at Bolobo, one of the gems of the National Congolese Army, a small place which the Belgians had turned into a model garrison for their police force in earlier

169

times. Bolobo is the gateway to the former province of Equateur, the only one of what was formerly the Belgian Congo to have escaped the hold of the rebels until the present time.

Katanga, Kivu, and the eastern province are partly occupied by the rebel groups who have made Kalemie their provisional capital, while other insurgent groups have settled in the provinces of Kinshasa and Kasai. There is no doubt that within a few hours the rebel troops should be joining forces in the province of Kasai. And, finally, there is the third front of the province of Equateur, the bridgehead in the region that was Graham Greene's setting for *A Burnt-Out Case*.

He decided to break the complete silence that had fallen.

"Mr. President, we knew all this. That is the reason we're here. We have to submit some suggestions for action to the President of the Republic as soon as possible. What do you propose?"

The President remained silent. He interpreted his silence as hurt vanity. Had he upset him that much? He yielded to the facts without wanting to: he had put himself in the spotlight. Now he wanted to recoil, put himself back in his place, to wait. The goal of sincerity that he had set himself had exposed him. Annoyed, he slightly bowed his head, as if he were acknowledging an error. He had dared to venture

170

down an unexpected road much too hastily. He thought to correct it by throwing out an empty but flattering remark.

"You know very well, Sir, that you are our only chance . . ."

Uneasy, he listened to an incoherent discussion about spying. His colleague had an impassive, faraway look on his face. That is what might be called a personality, he said to himself: the man has developed a talent for absenting himself which can only bring him friendship and sympathy. He seems to have neither a will, nor a voice, nor any opinions of his own. The President had let loose. He was demonstrating that the rebellion was essentially the act of a few ambitious government officials. In order to scale the rungs of power as rapidly as possible, they had found it expedient to rouse their tribes against the government in such a way as to be able to negotiate the price of peace. He was shouting.

"We cannot tolerate such blackmail . . . And, furthermore, with whom do we negotiate? We know that some foreign governments officially support the rebels. I don't exactly see how some renegade members of parliament can involve those governments and then expect to calm down a populace that's become fanatic . . ."

He tried to reflect. Some pragmatic conclusion, he thought, would have to follow these ranting preliminaries. The overall situation in the country seemed too serious to him to warrant its being settled by a lot of anticolonialist rhetoric. On the alert, he heard the speaker's tone change.

"We have sure indications that decisions we made

171

here, yes, here in our restricted meetings, are regularly transmitted to the rebels, and this even before we've put them into
action. That explains their so-called military successes . . ."

There were perhaps four or five of them who knew.
The explanation seemed too simplistic to him, too facile.
Were they looking for a scapegoat? Nice prospect, he said to
himself. He stiffened, stretched out his legs, convinced that
the game at hand was sheer lunacy, wondering how to act
upon the events in order to avert the ridicule towards which
the country was inevitably heading.

"Rationally speaking, the President of the Republic to
whom all our proposals are communicated, cannot be a suspect, nor those in charge of our National Army. . ."

His nerves taut, he was hanging suspended by the
shock waves coming on. There is a trap somewhere, he
thought. A wide-open trapdoor. But whose was it? And above
all, why? The President was justifying himself, swearing that
he himself had no contact whatsoever with the rebels, as
everyone knew. . .

"Moreover, the Chief of State and I myself know
your great honesty, your determination, your sense of the
State . . . it seems altogether unthinkable to us to imagine
that . . ."

In short, everyone was innocent, trust reigned supreme. Nevertheless, he was convinced that he had been tar-
geted personally. The discussion very obviously concerned
him. A plot, he said to himself. They want to sacrifice me.
He forced himself to remain indifferent, to seek the origin of

and the possible reasons for this attack. His eyes wandered from the French doors in front of him to an enormous painting that represented as abstract version of an owl. He was sure that, at this point in time, Security was discreetly digging into his life. A memory emerged. A warning which he had not noticed at all in time. It was about a week ago. He had gone to see the Master again.

"I have fulfilled all my obligations towards the ancestors and to the society. I've actually gone beyond the call of duty. Tell me why I have the feeling that everything breaks down the further I move forward . . ."

"You remain far too detached, my son. You lack faith. Any action, even the most disastrous one, could lead to happiness. The road to success is not always straight. You have some powerful enemies. Do not ever take them by surprise, but always be prepared to foresee their intentions."

"How would I know? How can I live in peace if I don't know what presages my anxiety, nor what accident might lead me to glory?"

"Our people have always said that only the unblemished heart survives."

"That is to say?"

"You have fulfilled your obligations, my son. Continue to do so and live according to the spirit of our Society. Don't ever forget that you are your own protector. Know that our people will continue to protect you as long as you don't fall from grace."

173

"How can one not be sinful, Master, when one's life is dedicated to public office?"

"I have told you how: never tarnish your soul and all will be permitted you."

He turned a cold look towards the President of the Council. He caught a startled curiosity on his face. He knew that he had to act. And firmly. He shuddered, then went at it:

"The problem is a complex one. In my opinion, it doesn't do us much good to devote all our time and energy just to searching for the person potentially responsible for the leak. That's a job for Security. The rebels are almost at the gates of . . ."

A vague cheerfulness passed over the President's features. I'm in a stable full of wild horses he said to himself. If I don't turn things around right now, I'll be trampled to pieces. Better to set the rules of power aside for now, and also the precedences of government, so that I can convince them first, rally them behind me.

"We can propose immediate measures centered around one important principle: create panic in order to control it. In concrete terms, we could first decide to arrest all politicians and merchants who have been in direct or indirect contact, close or otherwise, with the rebels . . . And I do mean all of them . . . Secondly, issue warrants for the arrest of those responsible in the tribal groups whose regions have presently joined the rebellion; and, at the same time, suppress all tribal groups which are a breeding ground for the cultivation of separatist feelings."

Images, seemingly unconnected, rolled by in front of his eyes. He no longer had time to link them: they collided, disappeared. She. Her sudden change. She was honest. But is it not possible to live a succession of honesties? Why would it have been necessary for him to refuse love under such a futile pretext? Of course, he knew that . . . But who doesn't do those things? He belonged to the race of princes, he was above any suspicion. She, Beauty, then, should be the same.

~

". . . and let's put all legalism aside. That's for later . . . Thirdly, from this day onward, we must proclaim a state of emergency in the troubled provinces, entrust the leadership there to military commanders endowed with special authority. . ."

Was she in danger? No. That's not possible. As long as I keep talking. Cover up for her. Of course, she was playing a crazy game, but one that didn't amount to much, on the whole . . . Furthermore, it was ridiculous. They had to be mad to believe that she could be responsible for the derouting of armies. It is the tribal network that needs to be dismantled.

". . . Fourthly, the national radio broadcasts should, from now on, announce the victories of our troops; they are to attack the enemies of the Nation, to crush them with hatred and contempt. Names? The foreign powers whom you just blamed earlier, Mr. President, some of the politicians to be arrested . . ."

He immured himself in violence. Calm, his voice lower than at first, he gave the impression that he was recit-

BEFORE THE BIRTH OF THE MOON

ing a lesson. He was watching his colleague seated in front of him, comfortably fixed in a motionlessness that was almost elegant. The Prime Minister, on the other hand, was consistently nodding his head in agreement.

". . . Finally, I propose that the plans for counterattack, decided by the specialists of the General Staff, be directly transmitted to the Chief of State for confirmation, without being processed by us. If you give me the authorization to . . ."

A pause. Faint sounds, then a woman's piercing scream rose up from the street. His voice hardened.

". . . I'd be pleased to volunteer. Accompanied by a few high-ranking officers, I shall take the new orders to the front in person. Officially, it might be said that I'm going on a mission to inspect the reconquered territories."

He thought he had shown the measure of his sense of protocol. Had he thwarted the trap? The President's protruding eyes had clouded over. But it was with a smile that he took the floor again.

"If you don't object, let's go over your proposals again, point by point; they seem very sound."

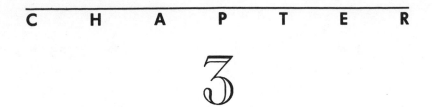

3

"You know, young lady, I am patient... Very patient in fact... And you'll end up by telling me the truth. So it might as well be now. For your own sake... Don't you want to eat? Sleep in a bed? Of course you do, don't you? So why not talk now..."

I was simply weary. Certainly, I yearned to eat, to sleep. And even more to wash up. My two-piece shantung suit was sticking to my body. And I didn't dare to think of the state of my underwear. I had waited for a miracle, but in vain. Incapable of knowing which way the wind was blowing, I had not budged from my earliest statement for forty-eight hours now, and I encountered the same questions with the same sense of powerlessness.

In a tan suit, a fine white shirt, silk tie, the Inspector, for two whole days now, had been parading such different faces before me that I no longer knew which one to trust. He was plumper than my musketeer. Taller as well. Sitting behind his desk, his look untroubled, he was cleaning his nails with undivided attention, exuding an air of goodheartedness. I was beginning to relax when suddenly he threw his nail file across the room and struck the table with a violent blow of his hand. He got up.

"So much the worse for you, if you don't plan to cooperate. In another hour, this whole affair is to be wrapped up. So . . . You understand?"

No, that was the point. I didn't understand anything. I was miserable, scrutinized him, losing myself in assumptions. For the hundredth time, I tried to get away from myself by focusing on my surroundings: the file trays that filled up the entire width of the desk, the bare light bulb dangling above his head, and to his left, more than six feet above the floor, the little window offering a small square of the clear night. Why is he interrogating me at night this time around?"

I had another hundred questions for him.

He roared:

"So, you're still determined to keep silent?"

I was thinking that I'd rather ask him whether reasons of State, and what reasons at that, could justify the treatment I was undergoing. They had come to get me out of bed two days earlier. And since then I'd been going from one interrogation to another on an empty stomach. I had told them everything. What could I possibly add? I was dead on my feet with exhaustion. The previous night I'd been allowed just four or five precarious hours of rest in a cell crammed with people.

"Let's finish this up, you rebel . . ."

He began the interrogation again, snares in every question. Since I had no idea what they were holding against me, I was paralyzed with fear. At this point, he was anxious to calm me down.

"Are you a member of that damned liberation movement?"

"No, sir."

Of course not, I told myself. If they were sure of their case, why would they come back to that point with such frequency?

"So, you solemnly declare that you don't belong to the movement?"

"Yes, sir."

"And yet, your father did belong?"

"Yes, sir."

179

"How do you know?"

"It was in the papers, sir."

Was he really listening to me? At any rate, he seemed most preoccupied fiddling with his cigar. In an absent-minded voice, he asked:

"Which papers? What date?"

"I really don't know any more. I did see it, though. And then, everybody was talking about it too. Even on the radio they said that my father was a rebel leader . . . I am unable to tell you any dates . . ."

And that was true. I no longer remembered the period in which the press had announced my father's death. I was sure, however, that I had seen articles on the subject. But not one of the inspectors believed me. Especially the one I was with now. He was looking straight at me with his little eyes. I thought of my famous uncle. Nerves taut, I waited for an outburst . . . However, it was in a very gentle voice that he said to me:

"You are lying, young lady. Not one single newspaper ever stated that your father was a rebel leader."

I was shaking with rage. Each time it was the same thing: a statement without any proof, but one that by a strange twist shredded my certainties to bits. There were moments where I would have begged him to charge me with something . . . I raised my eyes to him. He appeared distant, involved with his cigar . . . The first day I had mentioned something about a lawyer. He hadn't even bothered to answer me. Angry, I had made a scene, first insisting, then implor-

180

ing that I be permitted to phone my friend the Minister. Not for a single moment did he ever shed his quiet and distant contempt.

"Why him?"

"He is my friend . . . Notify him. You'll see . . . You will end up by apologizing to me."

"Is he really a friend of yours?"

"I'm telling you he is . . . We're going to be married soon . . ."

He had snickered with a detachment that staggered me. What was it that had occurred?

"Tell me, what was your relationship with the Minister?"

"I've already told you . . ."

The first time, his use of the past tense had baffled me. Even in the depths of my confusion, I placed myself in relationship to him. Maybe, I said to myself, his leaving town is in itself an explanation for my predicament. When he returns, he will clear me, will take my side. I couldn't allow this inspector to give himself the right to speak of my love in the past tense. The night before my arrest, he had told me that he would fly out very early the next morning on an inspection tour of the interior region. He had promised me that he'd return within ten days . . .

"That's not an answer, young lady."

"I've told you that I was his friend."

"You mean that you were one of his mistresses?"

He had gotten up and began to walk around me.

Anxious, I was trying not to give in: not to contradict myself. If I only knew the extent of the mire and what had become of my musketeer! The Inspector was standing in front of me.

"Explain this to me then: how is it that you, of all people, were his friend?"

"But, sir . . ."

I shrugged my shoulders. A blow crashed down on my cheek, cutting short a swear word I had on the tip of my tongue. How could he have guessed? I took the impact, jaws clenched.

"Be reasonable. It's pretty obvious that you're getting on my nerves. If you'd be nicer I wouldn't have to use violence . . ."

Taken aback by the sincerity of his tone, I was on the verge of accepting his apologies when he smacked me a second time, more brutally than before. I dissolved into tears.

He had sat down on the corner of the desk, was contemplating me with a jeering look. He was determined to run me into the ground.

"That's what happens to little girls who stick their nose in business that's not theirs . . . Now, let's begin again. And hurry it up . . . How do you explain your relationship with the Minister?"

"He was attracted to me . . . "

"When did you meet each other?"

"More than a year ago. In a bar."

"How long have you been living with him?"

"A few weeks . . ."

182

"Be specific . . . or else . . ."

"Almost a month, I think."

He had left the corner of the desk. He was pacing back and forth, smoking his cigar, eyes everywhere except on me. Unsuccessfully, I tried to think. His questions cut me off, opening one after the other breaches in a past that no longer deluded even me. I was convinced that I was cracking, but I waited, determined not to surrender until the Inspector showed his hand and then only if I felt truly doomed.

"Did he make a habit of talking to you about affairs of state?"

"Affairs of state?"

"Did he never mention the rebellion to you? Or measures taken by the government?"

"Yes. Sometimes he'd talk about it. But in general terms . . ."

"What do you mean, general terms?"

"Things that everybody knew, that I'd read in the papers also."

Perhaps it was the precise detail of the questions that made me think I'd figured it out at last. They suspect him of siding with the rebels. Perhaps they've already arrested him. And so I'm here as his accomplice . . . One thing I'd never thought possible. He, guilty? That was impossible. A pretext to break him. I smiled. My God, who could have told me a wilder story?

"What's so amusing?"

"Your questions, sir."

He thought this over, intrigued. He took two steps towards me, then stopped.

"What about my questions?"

"You seem to think that I'm a spy. Look at me carefully. Do I look like one?"

"I think nothing. I'm looking for facts. Did you know that your friend was one of the very few figures in the Republic who was in the know, particularly where it concerned all concrete political and military arrangements regarding the rebellious regions?"

"No."

"Tell me, then, how the rebels in charge were quite regularly informed, even before they happened, of all governmental arrangements?"

"How would I know? I really don't understand anything about these things."

"You're lying!"

He had screamed it. I heard the door open and close behind me: someone had come in. That mysterious presence behind my back terrified me. I was worried: What are they going to do to me? The rope was tightening, it was true. But would they dare to torture me? I desperately clung to the idea that they don't torture women. The Inspector had once again sat down on the corner of the desk. He was swinging his legs.

"You're cornered, you know. Check this: you admit that your father was a rebel leader, you tell me he was killed a few weeks ago . . . ; just by chance, during the same period, you become the mistress of a Minister of State who is known

184

for his irascibility against the insurgents, for his hatred towards your ethnic group . . . ; just by chance we notice that, as your love affair begins, before anything happens, the rebels have knowledge of all measures concerning them and are well-informed of the movements of our troops . . . Conclusion?"

"I assure you that you're wrong. I had been going out with the Minister for more than a year already . . . I loved him . . . I have never had any contact with the insurgents . . ."

"Then how did you know your father was a rebel leader?"

"I told you . . . Through the newspapers."

"You're lying. The newspapers announced his death. They never said that he was one of the heads of the rebellion . . ."

He was looking at me full of condescension. He came towards me, stopped behind the chair and put his hand on my shoulders. Gently he pressed down on them. Then he bent over me; he almost had his cheek against mine and I could feel the warmth of his breath. Instinctively, I saw a warning signal in this change of attitude. As I listened to him talk, I hardened myself.

"Listen to me, little girl, this whole business is ridiculous. You've been playing with fire, haven't you? Tell me so and I'll let you go . . . I swear . . . You would like a nice warm bath, wouldn't you?"

"I've told you the truth. You just don't believe me."

185

"Because you're taking me for an idiot."

He let go of me and stood to my left at an angle. I thought the time had come to defend myself. I was exasperated. I burst out:

"I don't know if you're an idiot. I only know that you believe in tribalism. Not for an instant did you believe it possible that I could live with this man because I love him . . . He is not of my tribe, therefore I cannot love him . . . And then, also, you haven't spent a minute trying to find out if it's one of your other ministers who . . . who . . . Why shouldn't it be my beloved Minister? He dreamed of power, didn't he? Are you so sure that it wasn't he who sold out to the rebels with the information? He stands protected by his rancor and his hatred. But me? . . . I'm the perfect choice for . . ."

I was gasping, liberated. Had I avoided some threat? I don't know what the pleasurable warmth was that went through me all of a sudden. What sort of preposterous idea was it to slander my musketeer like that? I felt no remorse. Without a word, the Inspector had gone to sit behind his desk again. He opened a drawer, took out a newspaper, held it up in front of my eyes.

"We don't suspect the Minister yet because of this."

Yes. It was clear. The words danced in front of my eyes, now dimmed with tears: a carnival of colors in which red and black reigned supreme.

186

ACCIDENT OR CRIMINAL ATTEMPT?
Minister burnt alive in car.
Leaving on inspection tour of province . . .
Great defender of the Nation . . .

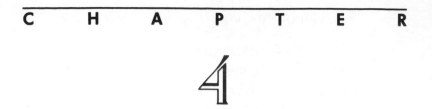

In the taxi that was taking me back to town, I tried to rejoice. At last I was going to be able to take a bath and to get some rest. In a day or two, if the landlord didn't evict me before then, I would move to another apartment, probably to a single room, to something less expensive. But my calvary continued. I dragged the last two days along

188

with me, and also the ghastly night from which I was just emerging, heavyhearted, crushed. When the jailers had come to take me away again, I was ready to surrender. Any prison at all, I told myself, would be more humane than this dungeon. I found the inspector crisp, close-shaven, smelling of cologne. He had put on a black suit that made him look like a businessman. Facing him, I felt dirty. He's a sadist, I said to myself as I came in. He just wants to humiliate me. I had stiffened intuitively, resolved to defend myself. It was unnecessary. He was coming towards me in anticipation, pulled a chair out for me. After that, everything happened very quickly.

"You are free to go, Miss. I'll call a taxi for you to take you home. But first you'll allow me to say two quick things to you. First, the Minister really loved you . . . and you are unworthy of him. The second I have to tell you is that you're one fine slut . . . Thanks to you, we do now have some strong presumptive evidence against him . . . Only, it's easy to charge a dead man. As far as I'm concerned, I'm still convinced that you had an understanding with the rebels . . . But here we are: you've presented us with a guilty person very suitable to a great many people . . . Let me just give you one piece of advice: take care not to fall into my hands again . . ."

It was the end of the tunnel. The taxi had arrived. The day had swung into action. I had left light-headed, despite the Inspector's scorn. What frenzy is letting me see it all again? I had had one sentence with which to protect myself. It had transformed itself into a breach, had permitted outra-

189

geous conjectures. All my musketeer could do was to accept serving me as a scapegoat, since he had loved me.

It was the Inspector whom I had learned to hate. For two days, he had knowingly hidden the fact of the musketeer's death from me. He had thrown those headlines in my face only to crush me. At the same time, he had sprung up out of his chair, had begun to scream:

"What do you say to that, huh?"

"Not a thing, sir."

I was under the impression that I was the victim of an error. He had gone plundering through my private life, skinning me alive, so that I might confess to a crime of which I knew nothing. Had I surprised him with my calm? What possible answer could I have given him? They were waiting for some comment. What could I offer them besides my grief? I loved him, this musketeer of mine. I had told them so from the beginning. And it was true. Did I have a hand in his death? Let them find some proof of that. It was their business. My own preoccupation now resided in an intense aggravation: I had been a cog in a machine and perhaps some of my excesses had designated me to become my own executioner. Was I really the one who had involuntarily decided his death by informing Ma Yene of the secret departure on an inspection tour? I had only my suffering as an expression of my neutrality in this battle. Hypocritically, the Inspector was pretending to be deeply grieved.

"Since you loved him, Miss, speak . . ."

"I have told you everything I know. From the very

start you were convinced that I was guilty. What do you want me to do?"

"Listen, young lady, you'd do well not to play any further games . . ."

His tone had been dry, low. I looked at him. His face showed the ferocity of a wild animal lying in wait for his prey. Savagely, he pulled out his drawer, took out some sheets of paper. A vicious pleasure spread over his face.

"I'm going to read you something that's addressed to you; a letter . . . We found it in his desk at the Ministry."

I said to myself: the axe is coming down on me at last. If he could have known . . . In despair I searched for the link that could possibly exist between my trips to the market and this letter, appearing out of nowhere. My tears saved me. Struck down in advance, I was waiting for the dead man's vengeance.

My friend,

My beloved friend, I'm leaving very early tomorrow morning and would like to think that, upon my return in about ten days, I'll find you in a happier state than you are now. Since we have been living together, I find you both close and far away. Close in a love which gives me more reasons every day to feel happy. Far away, so far away in some of your attitudes, that it seems as if you were observing me, particularly where it concerns certain questions that you pose, full of intense interest in political affairs. I understand all too well that the fate of your family worries you as long as they remain in one of the troubled areas. But is it really necessary to take on that look of apparent indiffer-

191

ence? Such an atmosphere can only bring unhappiness, I'm afraid. In this way, it often seems that you don't trust me; and for a while now, I've sometimes thought that you are only living with me for a specific purpose . . .

Extremely anxious, I was waiting for my doom. Inside my rib cage my heart was beating thunderously. Despite my tears, I made an effort to give my face a normal expression. It was useless. My head was bursting. I violently detested him now, my musketeer. What a foolish idea to leave me a letter when he could have spoken to me. With a smile on his lips, the Inspector was observing me.

. . . to be able to save your people when necessary, thanks to my position. Would that be all I am to you, simply your means to that particular end? I don't know where I stand exactly. But I love you enough to ignore it. So it is with pleasure that I can tell you now that, on my mission to the interior, I'll do everything within my power to meet your relatives and, if I can manage it, to take them out of that hornet's nest and bring them back to you.

This, because I love you and I'd do anything at all not to lose you. You have told me, and often tell me that you love me. You do understand, don't you, that I want to reach you, to know what is happening to us. In a way, our situation seems obvious: your coming back to me explained much. You begged me to find your friend for you and you were relinquishing yourself for that . . . With time, you found yourself falling in love, and I accepted you, the most natural thing in the world. You've asked me more than once to tell you why I love you . . .

I was beginning to catch my breath, imploring

heaven to let the danger pass, to let my fine musketeer get entangled in his emotions so that I might be saved. Despite the flashes of tenderness that rushed through me, I remained frozen in my terror.

... *For lack of rational reasons—if ever there are any in questions of love!—and since I have the time, I can offer you some explanation which, to my thinking, could clarify the attraction you hold for me. First of all, there is the simplicity of your being, of living, of thinking. You move around in a peaceable universe, made up of clear-cut certainties. Your openness to other people, your smile and your almost permanent good mood bespeak a spirit of innocence, of an inner peace that is genuine. In short, all the attributes I lack and that are missing generally in the big shots who fill governmental departments, in the haughty, and in the old matrons who frequent political circles. Then there is your availability. Physical and spiritual. You seem so trusting of others that you give yourself without any ulterior motive, without even seeming to suspect any ill will whatsoever in the other person. The goodness of your life seems to personify an extraordinary inner freedom. Finally, there is your body. You are the kind of woman of whom I've always dreamed: your large eyes, your naturally sensual mouth, your face which commands attention through its natural beauty. Your entire being is a hymn to womanhood; it is all the more remarkable because it stands in direct contrast to the young show-offs your age who try to mimic the male.*

I call you "Beauty." That's not merely a qualifier I bestow upon you; it is also the recognition of that wonderful harmony between your body and your spirit.

These three explanations obviously do not exhaust all my reasons for loving you. They fuse them. And I would so love it if you'd believe me and understand to what extent I am committed to you.

So let's drive away the shadows that have come between us. When I come back I would like so much to live with you without having to analyze myself at every turn. I say this because I leave with a troubled heart, troubled for the two of us, for our love. The last few times when I was with you, I had the uncomfortable feeling that my thoughts were being watched, my words studied. And that doesn't seem like you at all! I had even begun to cheat: my most innocuous words, like my gestures, were rehearsed, thought-out beforehand in order to see how you'd receive them. In other words, your presence forced me more and more to crush what little spontaneity I had just recovered thanks to you. I had even reached the point of fearing that I would betray what I consider the most beautiful thing you've brought me: that utmost tenderness that floods over me every time your look meets mine . . .

Spasms gripped my stomach. I was weeping for my good musketeer. I stood at the point where a whole series of coincidences converged. And more than ever, despite my sorrow, perhaps even because of it, I felt I had just cause to defend, against everything and everyone, the tributary's bed that I had dug. I opened my mouth to speak and discovered a taste of blood mixed with my tears. The Inspector, now standing, looked at me with disapproval.

"Now do you understand, Miss?"

"Yes, I understand."

"And?"

"It's a love letter."

"Is that all?"

"We were having some personal problems, that's all. He speaks of the rebels. It was he who was going to meet them, though, wasn't it?"

"You are a filthy whore, young woman. To vilify your..."

"I loved him, I swear."

I no longer dared to raise my face covered with tears. In humiliation, I felt the Inspector eyeing me contemptuously from head to toe.

"Do you still maintain you don't belong to some liberation movement or other?"

"Yes, I do."

One last night in the cell was still mine. With extreme coldness, I had reviewed all my actions and contacts of the past few weeks. I was certain: except for the letter's slight insinuations, I could find no mistake. What else could I do with this night that would not end? Fortunately, morning came again. I had crawled out of the abyss.

"Madame... Madame..."

The taxi had stopped. I paid the driver. Barely out of the car, I rediscovered the sun. It felt good. And the air. Swinging my purse with one hand, I jumped for joy, leaped up to the apartment with long strides, humming softly to myself.

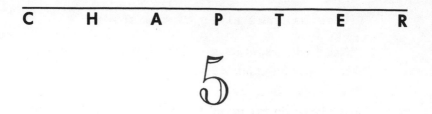

ou found the bar again. You had considered a change of location, but a kind of instinct led you back there. It was packed, as usual. One of the bartenders welcomed you with kindness, as if you were returning home.

196

"There you are, at last. Nothing new?"

"No. I'm fine. And yourself?"

"All right. But, like every Saturday night, the customers are getting on my nerves. You'll have a whiskey won't you? It's on the house."

The atmosphere was heavy. The air conditioners were set at high. Still, the crowd made running the machines almost useless. The orchestra was playing a soft melody. Suddenly the rhythm changed. You frowned, lips tightly closed. The lights were lowered. It was his favorite song. Was it pure chance, these blows struck at your temples? The bartender smiled at you pleasantly, his eyes sparkling with complicity. You ought not break the tradition of the middle of the night. It was the celebration of your return: you should, for the length of one dance, devote yourself to a memory.

"Will you dance with me, to celebrate my return?"

"Just as you wish, Miss."

You cleared a passage to the dance floor. He was slim, supple, with firm muscles. The singer smothered you. Blend in with this warm flow completely:

> *Silent sunlight, welcome in*
> *There is work I must now*
> *begin*
> *All my dreams have blown*
> *away*
> *And the children wait to play.*

197

Your hand crept up his back gently. You lightly touched his neck. You ought to, you thought, seal off the rainbows of another season.

"That's a lovely dress . . ."

"Thank you."

"What makes you so beautiful?"

You feel the pressure of his hands. They are moist. You moved your head back a little, gave him a blue-lit smile. How, indeed, did you manage?

"Nothing special, my friend. You just have to choose your dresses well . . ."

Yes, it was pretty, your little grey dress of fancy wool. Topstitching emphasized the edges of the long line of buttons. The straight neckline allowed you to wear a blue silk scarf, accentuating your short hair. The black belt, worn tightly, gives your narrow waist a simple elegance.

"And to preserve my looks, I dabble in politics . . ."

You felt his hands come and go on your back.

"What happened to your gentleman really is too bad . . . I saw it in the papers . . ."

"Yes, it's very sad."

"It seems that you've had some trouble with the police . . . Is that true?"

"Oh, no, not me. Why should I have trouble?"

Your partner dances on tiptoe, as if he were going to fly away. You look at the musicians. They seem sincere. Both their playing and the song seem to you a fugue in the wide sweep of heaven.

They'll soon remember things to do
When the heart is young
And the night is done
And the sky is blue
Morning songbird, sing away...

"Your gentleman's friend still comes here every night, you know... A lawyer. You know who he is, don't you? He usually arrives around one or two in the morning."

"I see. Thank you..."

At the counter you spotted a new girl, someone you didn't know. Perched on a barstool, wearing shorts, she was showing off the most beautiful legs, and the longest, you had seen in a long time.

"Who's that new girl?"

"I don't know her name, but I'll introduce you..."

He was holding you close. Together you formed a monstrous shadow, gaudy with color.

Lend a tune to another day
Bring your wings and choose a roof
Sing a song of love and truth
We'll soon remember if you do...

It was a bridge. You were coming home, the voyage ended. There will be no more storm, no more accident. It was enough for you to make a subtle adjustment. The song of

199

your return had been the song of your remembrance as well. It reconciled you with your image.

The dance ended, you thanked him. You went to kiss the musicians, then settled down at a good table, close to the dance floor. A few minutes later, an American joined you.

"Hello . . . we don't see much of you any more."

"Good evening . . . Well, here I am again!"

You picked things up where you had left them. A waiter brought your drinks. The American took off his corduroy jacket, loosened his tie. As you had expected, his hand, open and hot, immediately accosted your legs. He was fidgeting.

"What happened to you, my girl?"

"Nothing. Nothing at all. Why do you think something happened to me?"

He was attending to you like an old, depraved uncle. You let it go, sad, knowing you no longer had any reason to reject him. You were a dirty river, as the musketeer had told you. That was about a week before his death. He had come home from the office earlier than usual, had dashed into the apartment.

"Take it easy today, Beauty. No appointments tonight. Come, let's go and dream by the river . . ."

He had taken you away in the car. It was ridiculous: the river was hardly a mile away and walking would have done him good. He had stopped the car on the circular road. You'd gone down to the bottom of a staircase which brought the water within reach. He sat down on the ground and you were waiting for him to speak.

"My musketeer is tired?"

It was more of an acknowledgement. He answered in the same tone, but distantly.

"Yes, Beauty, very tired."

You had taken his hands. They were cold. You had tried to relax him: you had stretched out on the step in such a way that you could put your head on his knees. You were waiting for him to see your face, which you were turning towards his. His eyes remained lost in the distance.

"My musketeer is very tired, very very tired . . . He ought to rest for at least a week . . . I'll spoil him in all sorts of ways . . ."

"Thank you, Beauty . . . I'm looking at the river . . . It is dirty but strong. And I'm thinking that we, we too . . ."

He was hesitant. You wanted to come to his rescue.

"We too . . . what, my musketeer?"

He had leaned over you. His eyes in yours, he had murmured very rapidly, as if he were afraid:

" . . . we too are dirty rivers, but we aren't strong, not strong at all."

You had expected him to lead up to an important revelation. Nothing followed. He had kissed you tenderly. An hour later, when it was dark, you'd gone back to town.

You study your American, wondering if you're going to keep him all night or leave him to entertain the lawyer who should be coming any moment now. You drink the glass of whiskey in your hand, hoping to find the self-confidence and the security necessary for your protection tonight. He is nice enough, the American.

"What's your name?"

"Thomas."

"Thomas?"

"Yes. Thomas Reeves . . . You can call me Tom. And what's yours?"

"They call me Ya."

"Ya?"

"Yes. It means sister. That's the name I like."

He laughed, pleased. This was your chance, you thought, to hook him and yet keep him at a distance.

"Are you still a technician?"

"Yes, indeed, still am."

"What do technicians do?"

"It's very complicated to explain. But in a few words, I help your country to develop itself. You see?"

No, you did not see. All you needed was his presence to make it till two o'clock. He was attractive.

"You're good-looking, my technician."

"Really?"

"Yes, really. Entertain me. All right? Come, let's dance . . ."

AUTHOR'S NOTE

The story takes place in Kinshasa, capital of the Republic of Zaire, formerly named the Democratic Republic of the Congo. The speech of the President of the Republic, excerpted in part 4 of section II, was delivered in the Palais de la Nation by M. J. Kasa-Vubu, Chief of State, at the opening of the first federal session of the second legislature, on October 7, 1965. The insurrection, mentioned throughout the story, has as a basis the rebellions which did, in fact, take place. (See B. Verhaegen, *Rébellions au Congo*, Études du C.R.I.S.P., Brussels, 2 vols.). The excerpt from the press, cited in section IV, part 2, appeared in *Le Monde*, on July 30, 1964, under the byline of P. De Vos. I have intentionally distorted it.

That which I have taken from history ends here. The story as well as its characters are fictitious; any resemblance to real events or people can only be coincidence.

A last remark: the cannibalist farce is imaginary, from beginning to end. The ritual litany, however, is from a Nkundo prayer. In its proper cultural context it has nothing to do with human sacrifice. (See V. Mulago in *Les Religions Africaines comme Source de Valeurs de Civilisation*, Présence Africaine, Paris, 1972, pp. 134–35.)

203

ABOUT THE AUTHOR

V. Y. Mudimbe is Professor of Romance Languages and Comparative Literature at Duke University, North Carolina. He has published more than sixty articles, three collections of poetry, four novels, and nonfiction books in applied linguistics, philosophy, and social science. He received the Grand Prize, International Catholic Literature in Paris in 1975 for his novel, *Entre les Eaux*, and the Senghor Grand Prize of the French language Writers Association in Paris in 1977 for all his published works to date.